SUNGAZER

**Books
by
Gerald Hausman**

GUNS
Turtle Dream
Ghost Walk
Tunkashila

STAR SONG *series*
Evil Chasing Way
Hand Trembler
Sungazer

**Coming Soon!
STAR SONG**
Hail Chanter - Book 4

SUNGAZER

GERALD HAUSMAN

SPEAKING VOLUMES, LLC
NAPLES, FLORIDA
2018

Sungazer

Copyright © 2018 by Gerald Hausman

ISBN 978-1-62815-950-9

To Mackie McDonnough

Acknowledgments

Grateful thanks to Mike Gleeson,
Michele Scott, and everyone at Blue Harbour

"River stone down bottom don't feel hot sun on top."
—Jamaican Proverb

Chapter One

Tesuque, New Mexico, 1985

Al-lan had given up his guise as a dog and taken on a man suit. He looked normal to me but every now and then he seemed, out of the corner of my eye, to be an insect. A great green insect whose body was a husk of greenish chlorophyll.

He read my mind. He was good at that. What he said was, "One time Locust showed me how to use a chunk of mica schist. He put it over his open eye, usually his left, and stared at a star, or sometimes, the sun."

"What did that do?" I asked.

"It gave him powers."

"Powers of sight?"

Al-lan nodded. "Powers of flight, too."

He then stood in a sort of statuesque pose. Arms outstretched, as if preparing himself for flight. He was all-over green, as if painted, and suddenly his arms began to spin, to rotate. I saw that they had turned to filamented gauze with blue veins. He was no longer a man. He was a giant insect. A locust.

"Put your hands on my shoulders," he said. His voice echoed in the wind.

I did as he said.

He began revolving into the surrounding darkness.

I revolved with him, the wind screaming in my ears.

The black jaws of a giant canyon opened below us as we spun.

With my mind more than my body I held on to him and when he floated away, etherized by the cool windy dark, he turned into a tiny spark of an insect.

Then he was gone and I was alone, floating.

I was falling into a terrible void. Endless in its vacuity. It was like an engulfing maw seeking to devour me. I let it swallow me. I forgave myself the fear of weightlessness. The complicity of nothingness. The utter loss of self.

I dropped, and dropped. And disappeared.

Chapter Two

As I fell, as I dropped into infinity, I understood only that there was no sun, moon, stars, or earth. But gradually I came to know that there was light, if ever so small.

There was a blade of light below me, thinner than hope, more meager than belief.

But as I believed in it and hoped for it and fell toward it, I saw that it was blue dawn coming towards me.

I continued to fall. But by now it did not seem I was falling but rather something, the flat darkness, was moving up to me.

The blade of light toward the west was now yellow dawn and I could see it well. Soon though this too changed, as I turned like a dark star, to meet it.

Now it was white dawn, four fingers high, still a knife-like light.

There was a sheath below it, as if it had pulled itself free of that sheath.

I realized then there were many dawns beneath me—possibly four in all.

It seemed I was falling through four mornings, but night was still a belt of darkness.

I continued my downward flight and now I could feel the omnipresence of up-thrust wind against my chest.

And the sound of water filled my ears.

The blade of light was now a sword, banishing the darkness.

And I saw four mountains. They were coming up as I was coming down.

There was a white mountain to the east, a blue mountain to the south.

There was a yellow mountain to the west, a black mountain to the north.

And I was the pinwheel, the dark star falling, in the center of this upward and downward movement.

If I was afraid, I did not know it.

I heard rushing waters moving upward. The waters frothed. The whitish tips of waves could be seen. They rose to meet me. But they only whitened my tail feathers. The foamy waters painted them white. I knew then that I was the bird known as Turkey.

I was on the top of black mountain and I scurried now through a hole, a cave and went even higher. I moved as fast as I could to get above the rising waters. But they moved faster than I could, and I knew I would soon drown.

I moved into the upper air as quickly as I could. But in the end I came to the impasse of total darkness again. The dark belt above me was like rock. The waters rose and whitened my tailfeathers some more. I gobbled in fear. I was afraid to be extinguished.

Then in a flash of gold light I saw the one who was Locust. He had a bow of illumined darkness flickering with little lightnings. I knew him from before. He had a quiver full of arrows and a bow of brightness, and he now loosed the arrows one at a time.

And the arrows tore through the night sky overhead and ripped an opening there and light poured in to meet the foamy froth of waters below, and those waters receded and Locust laughed. He swung his bow of dark light all round him and the mountain grew wider and the waters receded and we stood together in the light of bitterness, brightness, the light of man and woman and budding leaves and falling leaves and all the animal people that ever were or will be.

And that was Locust.

And he put down his bow and came forward.

And pecked me on the lips.

Chapter Three

I had hand trembled so many times that by now I was used to doing it in my sleep. It wasn't different from dreams or dreaming. But it was dimensionally different. Not two-d, three-d. You could feel the fullness, the reality of that. There was a kinetic reality to hand trembling that differed from dreaming. I suppose it was called lucid dreaming by psychologists, when all that you experience in the dream state becomes even more prescient.

The experience with Locust was like that. Was it really Al-lan?

Had he really kissed me on the lips?

I found out soon enough.

I'd fallen asleep in our upstairs bedroom. The connecting bathroom has a chute that draws cool air into the house in summer and circulates warm air in winter. It also draws centipedes into the house and sometimes birds.

As I came into wakefulness, I felt the bird on my chest.

So, it wasn't Al-lan, Locust, it was a magpie with a glittering rosy-centered eye. Its feathers were black and white and the black had a blue-green cast. I reached out and gently confined the magpie with soft hands. It made clicking and popping noises in its throat.

I carried the beautiful bird outdoors and down the hill to the aspen where it had a nest. I knew the magpie wanted to tell me something. I learned quickly enough what it was. A nestling had fallen from the mishmash tangle of stray branches that formed the haphazard nest above my head. By stepping on a boulder that leaned against the aspen tree, I could get to the messy magpie nest and thus deposited Mom. Then I went below to the sandy arroyo and got baby. Baby was all downy plumage with an outsize head that wobbled on a pink stalk of neck.

There is nothing like a magpie in the morning before the first sip of coffee.

There is nothing like doing some good in the world while the world is still young in your wakened mind.

Mom magpie circled me four times as I walked back up to the house. She croaked thanks.

I croaked welcome.

Then coffee with Laura. Strong black coffee. Looking into her green eyes, I knew why the world was young and why we walked in beauty, in *hozhonii*, as Ray Brown always said.

"Next year we will have been together twenty years," Laura said. "Let's go for another twenty."

She laughed, sipped her coffee. "You and your trembling," she said, chuckling.

"What if we both trembled?"

"Not me."

She was Scots-Irish, mostly. Her world view is prescribed by that predictable begin-middle-end that Aristotle talked about.

My Romany roots allow me to dream on, whether asleep or awake. All and everything will go on for as long as forever is.

In my mind, I would always be alive.

And so therefore would she.

Chapter Four

"If everything is made up of your bullshit magic," my friend Moccia used to say, "some world it would be!"

"Is," I told him.

This argument of ours started in the playground of Columbia School in 1955.

And here it is, thirty years later, and he is out in San Diego somewhere, hissing at those who think the world is anything other than solid matter, with its collisions and corruptions of what Hamlet decried— "this too-too solid flesh."

Fortunately, my friend Moccia was tempered back in the bad old days by another friend named Fred.

Fred and I are still friends. We see things others don't see. And though Fred is biased by science, but he also sees ghosts. We don't argue. Why should we? Under different circumstances, we see the same things. Once he found an ancient Pueblo ax head and gave it to me for a present. I kept it in a nicho for years and one day he asked for it back. I gave it to him. He returned it to a kiva at Jemez Pueblo. Fred's mystic friend said, "I knew it would come back some day."

That is how we see things. Things come and go. Life circles and spirals.

So it's not surprising that one day Fred asked me to go to the old Manby hot springs outside of Taos, New Mexico. "To see and to feel the spirits that dwell there."

I knew all about Arthur Manby, the notorious devil-saint who planted the cottonwoods on the sidewalks of Taos, who stole the land grant properties of hundreds of Hispanic farmers and resold them to others in the 1920s, who was thought to be a man of power not wholly confined to real estate and cottonwood trees, who had his head cut off while he lay in bed contemplating his rise to rule, his kingly command over the lands he had stolen.

The body of Manby was never identified—no head, no dental records, no features of face or fingerprint—and the Taos County records say that those who knew believed that Manby's dog had devoured his head. This all happened so long ago that it's all legend, myth, according to Frank Waters. But he says in his book *To Possess the Land* that Manby was later seen in London walking gingerly down the street.

My wife's family, the Wrights, settled in Taos in the 1880s. They had a ranch that ended up in the possession of DH Lawrence. That's another story. But they sold the ranch to Arthur Manby in 1908. The same one who lost his head.

And now Fred, my elementary school pal, was taking me down an old coach road to an overlook by the Rio Grande Gorge where we would camp for the night after steeping ourselves in Manby's ancient haunted hot springs.

We steeped and soaked and the old stones sang in the twilight and Fred and I caught and ate trout and cooked them over a sage-stoked fire and then slept under the stars.

That night the rumble of iron wheels woke us and a stagecoach rumbled out of the chamisa and plumes of desert dust were cast into the starlit heavens as Manby's coach thundered by. We barely had time to get out of the way.

I had horse lather on my forehead and the dust adhered to it. I smelled Manby's pipe smoke and heard him curse as he whipped his six horses. And then as sudden as it came, it was gone.

Life is like that.

Magpie in the morning.

Ghost coach at night.

Three days later Fred and I were in a Seri Indian cave in the Mexican Baja.

Chapter Five

The cave was not a secret to the Seri.

They lived within the secret. They were the secret. As Fred explained it, driving through Hermosillo with the salt air penetrating the VW bus, it was all about the Mother and Child. The Virgin of Guadalupe and the people themselves.

"We are all children," Fred said, "looking for our mother."

I said nothing, thinking about this. Then he added, "The Mother is here in these sea-bent hills. I'll show you. But it's just as Robert Boissiere said, the cave is here, too, as he said."

Robert was a mutual friend of ours. He was a Frenchman who in the 1940s had gone to Hopi and become one with them. He was the only white man I'd ever met who was not only allowed to live at Hopi but was permitted to take part in their ceremonies.

He once shot an arrow to the sun, a prayer to the Sun Father, and was answered by rain that broke a drought. At this writing, Robert is a spirit. But the cave where he said he found enlightenment was the one Fred was taking me to. I had never been there before.

The cave was at the very edge of a cliff.

We jogged to it. Fred was a great runner. Once, when I was in the 9th grade, he beat me in the 400, and I never forgot the surge of his victory. A year later, when we were 10th graders, I beat him at intramural wrestling. We were even. And so, best friends for life.

Now we were seekers of the grail, so to say.

Fred knew well how nervous I was on escarpments. I got myself into trouble on one climbing excursion with him. We were in the Grand Canyon and I froze on the sheer cliffs of Mooney Falls. Fred's son, Brendan, only five, sort of sprinted past me, vertically. There was a chain you could hold onto as you ascended but Brendan, like Bugs Bunny in a cartoon, vaulted past me. I got the shivers, looking down into the depths of the little canyon, and Fred talked me out of fear, showing me that holding on so tight to the chain was going to keep me there forever. He gently urged me upward, hand over hand, until we reached the top.

This was different. Also worse. The cliff offered no hand hold. The pounding surf below creamed over the black rocks on the tiny beach. We were maybe 60 feet above the sea negotiating a crevice. A four-inch ledge. I leaned into the safety of the rock wall. Fred, once again, eased me upward and then straight across a bridge of stone twelve inches wide. Then we were there and the cave ushered cool dry air into our faces.

Inside it was illuminated by hundreds of candles. Offerings of feathers and ornaments, letters scrawled on parchment-like, sea worn paper, baby shoes so old they could have been made of paper, bracelets, wrist watches, pocket watches, photographs—thousands of them pinioned by stones of all sorts and kinds, clothing, shirts and boots, moccasins, mantillas, capes, faded blue jeans, cement and mud-stained work pants, hats of every kind imaginable but mostly woven of straw, wedding clothes of formal style, dried flowers, mostly roses flowing out of the walls, but ancient orchids dried to cardboard consistency so that if you touched them they would have disintegrated.

"You have something with you that you want to leave," Fred whispered.

I nodded. I had the bag given to me by Sungazer. Half of the sacred feathers were in there, the other half were hanging on my clear-story mud wall at home in Tesuque.

I extracted the feathers and placed them on a metate.

The same moment I took my hand away from them, the candles in the cave, the shrine of the Virgin of Guadalupe, guttered and danced.

Outside in the sun and surf I heard the cormorants coughing.

The gulls cried.

An eagle, very high up, whistled a staccato warble.

Then, the wind came up and played around the little golden room.

But the candles didn't go out.

It took us a few hours to get back to camp.

My legs felt stronger for the climb, but more-so, for the gift of light I received in the cave.

We ran, soft-footed and slow for many miles and the sky darkened and night came on. Neither of us spoke. Our hands moved gentle as tropical leaves at our sides as we jogged.

We were barefoot. Our running shoes tied loosely around our neck.

The desert seemed so still. It emitted no sound.

We ran in silence. In darkness.

Then off to my left a saguaro cactus suddenly burst into flame.

Bright orange tendrils of fire leaped off it.

It was the very symbol of burning man.

For a while we stood and watched it as the sweat froze on our skin.

Finally, Fred spoke. What he said was a poem.

On December 9, 1531
The Virgin Mother of the Americas
Appeared before the face of a Nahuatl man.
'What do you want?' he asked her.
'I want you to tell the Bishop
That I have come to watch over
my children for all time'.
'Am I your child?' he asked.
'Yes, I am your mother
And you are my child,
So shall it always be.'

We ran back to our camp and I felt the cactus burning in my heart.
I still do.

Chapter Six

We drove back through the heat and dust of Hermosillo, turned north and drove straight to Arizona.

I kept seeing the elongated spiny arms of the cactus flaming in the starry Baja night. Aside from something miraculous, what could set a cactus on fire? Nothing that I knew of or could imagine. I left it as a prophecy of the miraculous in honor of Fred's son and my student, Dan.

Dan had been smashed pretty bad by an auto accident and was now limping along but still holding firm to his dream of becoming one of the fastest runners of the 1500 meters in the U.S.

But the dream frayed from time to time, as dreams will. Yet the incendiary cactus as a defiant and exultant version of Dan. Left arm raised, finger pointing to heaven. On fire.

It would come to pass, I knew.

But going back through the desert, I only knew half of it. Time would tell. I didn't know then that the burning part meant victory, and destruction. Can you have one without the other?

We camped, Fred and I, on the banks of Clear Creek in Central Arizona.

He found, as he often did, a large collared lizard.

We ate red chile in his camper and watched the sun go down.

We swam in Clear Creek. Trout bumped at our bare feet and Fred hand-caught and cooked it over a campfire of sage. Then, at dusk we walked along the river with its tamarisk trees fanning in the wind. There were thorn trees and dwarf oaks and we climbed up the steep slope that pointed northwest.

There was a moment where my old nemesis centipede crossed my climbing path. I was flat out in a crawl when the creature sprang up in front of my face and clacked its fangs. I could almost smell its poisonous intention. I jerked my head back and Fred, seeing all of this behind me, said, "Give it room."

I could do that, backing up quick, but I knew I might fall to the river rocks.

I lowered my head and the centipede, larger than life, crawled through my hair, paused at my neckline and went to my shoulder where it veered off into the bed of dried oak leaves. I heard it clicking away, ticking away into the shadows.

Fred said only one thing: "Close call."

Back at camp night had settled in, staining the sky blood red at the rim of mountain and stars. Fred made coffee. And afterwards we went into dark Clear Creek and swam by moonlight. The desert night was hot but climbing out of the water, we both shivered, and laughed.

We let the moon-breath desert air, dry us off.

Standing in that milky light, I repeated what Fred said earlier. "Close call."

Fred added, "That thing was six inches long. Desert centipedes grow large in these isolated places."

"Have they any natural enemies?"

He mused for a moment, smiling. "Hawks, lizards like the one I caught with the white collar and green skin, the occasional tortoise, magpies, usually two at a time picking at head and tail, quick with scissor beaks. Coatis, too."

"What are coatis?"

"Ringtail cats."

"The ones with the upright, flagpole tails?"

"Right." He chuckled. "I expect we'll see some tonight. I saw their dens earlier. They live like prairie dogs in a sort of sand village."

Before we got into our sleeping bags, we did see a few. In the dense overlay of moon and bush, we saw a tribe of these little people. Young and old. Their catfaces half dog as well, and their eyes large and luminous. Their hands—not really paws—looked human. The way they stood upright amused us. Perfectly straight little ramrods with that long ringed tail behind them, like air hoses of a Tom Swift interplanetary space explorer.

I went to sleep thinking about how their chortle was almost language. Almost conversation.

And woke suddenly from a dream.

A coati was standing, narrow-shouldered, bright-eyed, right next to me.

The coati whispered. "You know who I am."

It took me a moment. But I recognized him. He actually smiled with his curving jaw and little white teeth. In the moon he looked almost human. But his voice was clear and unaffected. It was my old friend Al-lan.

"Look at you," he said in a mocking voice. "You've hand trembled in your sleep."

I glanced at my hand; it was a paw. More dark hand than five-fingered animal digits, I thought.

Fred was asleep. He wouldn't have liked this. So we, Al-lan and I, wandered out into a moony field of datura blossoms.

"Dessert," he said.

"Do you mean desert?" I asked.

"No," he answered. "I mean we'll eat those for our dessert. Right now we're going to have some crispy centipedes for our main course."

"You're crazy."

"No. Just extraterrestrial."

He explained then as we sat on what looked like ceremonial stones, bathed in moonbeams, that centipedes were a delicacy that Xerxians craved. "They're good for humans, too," he said. "Oh-so-full of proteins you can't find anywhere else. Their poison is good for you too."

"Are you telling me that a centipede's bite is not dangerous?"

"For you or me?"

"For me."

"Well," he laughed. "You're not you right now, are you?"

I looked again at my extra-long opposable thumb, my long thin fingers with their noticeable knuckles.

"I guess I am what I am," I said. "In this extended, shape-shifting, dream of life, anyway."

"Well," he added, "Care to try?"

He held a quivering, furious mad centipede between his first finger and thumb. "Come to Mama," he said, and dropped the wriggling, clicking insect into his mouth. He crunched it like crackerjacks. Then wiped his linear jaws with the back of his delicate hand-paw.

"Go ahead," he said. "Once snack, never back." He laughed at his own silliness. "Actually," he said, "You eat one and after that you will never be bitten by one."

I thought about it. Al-lan was never wrong about the things he knew. In a quick fit of inspiration—and imitation—I picked up a writhing, live centipede and dropped it into my mouth and hurriedly crunched it, armored body tickling down my throat along with frantic arms, legs, antennaes, fangs and who knows what.

"There," Al-lan said with satisfaction, "now for some sacred datura."

Chapter Seven

He took me to a nearby field, flat as a pancake. There were even flat, pancake-like stones between which grew these weird, elegant flowers.

"Be careful with these," Al-lan told me.

"Why?"

"Because ringtails can fall over dead if we get too much blossom in us. Whatever you do, don't eat the flower or the plant. It's very potent, maybe poison."

I sighed. Al-lan was always the emperor of punchlines.

"You've seen this, I suppose."

"Yes, I've seen big, fat cows go crazy. I saw one fall over dead from too much datura. It's sweet stuff. That's why the hawk moths go for it. See them?"

I looked around in the pale moonlight and there were, just as he said, hundreds of furry moths hovering like hummingbirds.

It was a dizzying sight.

Al-lan sniffed a trumpet-shaped flower and said, "Ahhhh."

"What's it smell like?" I asked.

His dark eyes brightened and almost seemed to glow.

"Smells like…hmm…"

"Yes?"

"…like…"

He seemed dazed.

"Like?"

He shook his head. I thought I saw a faint corona of golden pollen around his nose but it was probably my imagination.

"Smells like something sweet, narcotic, erotic, heady, soapy, per-fumey."

Al-lan was quiet for a moment while his whiskers flashed like needles in the moon. He shook his head. "That said, my friend, trust me, datura pollen in the nose of a ringtail cat is more than a smell…it's a spell!"

"Not sure I want to try it," I said.

"Oh, you have to. I don't like doing it alone. Besides, you're a hand trembler, you can always tremble out of it if you need to."

I agreed that was true. But I still wasn't sure. Yet, watching the hawk moths blur about the field, obviously intoxicated, made me want to try.

"Maybe just a sniff," I said cautiously.

He smiled and the silver white moon gleamed and his eyes danced.

I bent down to one orchestral trumpet of a flower.

As I did so several moths blew past and hung over my head.

It was as if they were saying, "Go ahead. Have a turn."

So I did. One tentative sniff.

The floral tube of the flower allowed my nose to go in deeper than I wanted it to but when I pulled it out, I had a little taste of the ineffable. It was, for sure, an indescribable thing. No fragrance, really. But the immediate effect was a sexy one.

Al-lan was observing me. "Don't get any ideas," he said.

I rolled a time or two in the dust and felt much better. Then I came back to another flower. It seemed to beckon.

There was a moment or two when the air smelled like fresh roasted peanuts. Another time, it seemed the night was raining a gentle dust of cocoa and lavender. The moths hovered like haloes over my head. The pollen was powdery on my face and the air was smoky with that ineluctable, hallucinatory smell.

"Do you miss your mother?" Al-lan asked.

"Has it come to that?"

"My first time I missed my mother something awful."

"I never knew you had one."

"Everyone has one."

The next thing I knew I was in my sleeping bag and it was early morning.

Fred was there next to me, asleep.

I looked for Al-lan. He was nowhere to be seen.

Then in the soft beige sand there was a one-finger drawing of a smiling ringtail.

I chuckled.

Then I looked at my hands.

They were long and furry and tapered.

I felt the rest of me.

I was still human.

Everything…

but the hands.

Chapter Eight

The fingertips were calloused. The nails were long, and sharp.

Might be useful someday, I mused.

Then: What the hell am I saying? I've got to get rid of these things. But how?

I took a deep breath.

And remembered the datura. I was still high. I actually couldn't feel my body. But I could feel the tiny lichen-like fur all over the tops of my hands. My palms were black and wrinkly. I made a fist. It wasn't all that strong. I thumped my chest once. Then I picked up a bit of mesquite lying by my sleeping bag.

I pinched it with my right and then my left. Mesquite is resilient. I bent the stick and it snapped instantly. I then pressed my fingertips together and pushed as I was taught in my Tibetan martial arts class. It was an isometric exercise that measured finger strength. I felt the tingle of power course through the digits.

My fingers were strong. Very strong.

I closed my eyes and saw the field of flowers. Moon white and lavender pale.

I breathed deeply.

Fred was crouched near me. He had two coffee cups.

"What the hell were you just doing?"

"Nothing," I said, accepting the hot coffee. "Just an exercise."

"Is that what gave you those hairy hands?"

"It's an orgone cream I have been using. Jack Kerouac used to use it."

Fred sipped his coffee and continued to crouch, Pueblo style.

"Some hands," he said, shaking his head. "Do you stretch the ligaments, too?"

"Somewhat."

"Good in a bar fight?"

I sipped my coffee which had a burned mesquite taste.

"They're like scissors," I told him.

"How come I didn't notice them before?"

"It has to do with the moon."

"You trying to tell me you're a werewolf?"

"More like a sort of werecat. Just the hands."

"And because of the what-did-you-say…orgon?"

"Orgone."

"How does that work? Not that I want to try it."

Fred disappeared into the van and brought out a slightly crunched box of day-old doughnuts. "Dip 'em in the coffee," he recommended.

I did that thing.

The light of day made my coati hands look prickly. Ate my soggy doughnut. It tasted good.

The light on the salt cedars was buttery and gold.

Wind riffled the green waters of Clear Creek.

"You have any gloves, Fred?"

"You don't want people seeing those, do you?"

"Would you?"

He said, "I'll be right back. Don't go padding off somewhere, OK? Some goofy hunter's liable to take a shot at you. How're your feet, by the way?"

"Normal. Just like yours."

He returned a moment later with a pair of yard gloves, the kind that have a weave to them, allowing the gloves to breathe. "I use these for lifting lightweights," he said. "You know to warm up before a run."

I set my coffee on a flat rock and put on the gloves.

Right away I felt better.

A crazy poem ran through my mind. I'd written it years ago, I don't know why.

The poem was called *Handyman* and it went something like this:

> *Well, I gotta hand it to you,*
> *But first let's have a show of hands…*
> *Why doesn't he just hand it over?*
> *I guess one hand washes the other…*
> *We caught him all right, red-handed, too…*
> *Ah, they're just hand-me-downs…*
> *Hey, gimme a hand, will ya?*
> *Two hands are better than one!*
> *Now isn't he handsome?*
> *The sound of one hand clapping…*
> *The sound*
> *Of*
> *One hand…*

Chapter Nine

We packed up to go. I said goodbye to Clear Creek and its dwarf oaks, its odd, bent Russian olive trees, its centipedes. I thought of those many-footed six-inch nightmares, and especially the one that did the face-off with me.

I realized I'd been so stoned the night before that I'd just dropped my jeans and rolled them up into a flat pillow. As I tugged them on I felt the dew on the denim.

And then I felt something else.

It was a tickle, at first. Right around the groin.

I let the jeans drop ever so slowly.

Something was in my jockey shorts.

And somehow I knew what it was.

I dropped my shorts with infinite care.

Tangled up in my pubic hair was another giant red-brown centipede.

I said a silent prayer and flicked it out of there.

Surprisingly, my pincer-like fingers caught the creature.

I held it in the air for a second or two.

"You didn't bite me, so I'm not going to bite you."

Then I flung it into some cottonwood leaves by the creek and it rattled away.

"Those Sonoran centipedes are really long," Fred said, as he rolled up his bedding and tied it with a short piece of hemp. "So now I see another use for the furry hands, partner. They can clip on to things really fast, can't they?"

"I don't know. That's the first time, for me."

My heart was still racing, but I was aware that the hard knock heart suddenly dropped a beat or two and resumed its steady easy rhythm.

There were things going on inside me that had never gone on before. Datura? Or some spell of Al-lan's?

Fred started the van. "You coming?" he asked with a sly grin.

We crossed the river seven times going back to the main road.

At the last turn, Fred said, "One more swim?"

I nodded. It seemed like a good idea to wash off the night sweat, the datura haze in my head.

But before we could do anything, we heard a woman scream.

Between a boulder and a warped gray cedar, a woman with a top-heavy backpack was floundering. Fred and I raced over to where she was thrashing her arms, and then without a sound, she sank like a stone.

I went under fast, swam through the clear green and grabbed her ankle. We were in about twelve feet of water but the current was slow in this spot and I had a good hold of her knee with my right hand, and with my left, I had a finger lock on her ankle. My eyes were open underwater, but I could see as clear as if I were a fish. The woman had been down about a minute now, I was counting fingers in my head.

The problem was that her feet were lodged in a fissure. She was deeply wedged in. Fred swam around her and then dived again and got hold of her backpack, which must have weighed eighty pounds. It had pots and pans hanging off it, a hand axe and some other effluvia.

The pack lifted. Fred had it off her.

I pulled her ankles at the same time, he lifted off the pack.

The grip of my gloved hands was hard to believe.

I raised the woman straight out of the water and shoved her forward to the river bank.

Then all three of us lay on the matted river grass and just breathed.

Strangely, I seemed not to be winded.

I turned my head and looked down into the water where I saw a glitter.

I swam down and got it—the woman's watch.

I could see underwater perfectly, as if I had a swim mask.

When I surfaced she was babbling to Fred about how we'd saved her life.

"Why was your pack so full?" Fred asked.

She had big blue eyes and she blinked several times and drew in more oxygenated river air. "I made a mistake," she gasped between breaths.

"You're right about that."

"Are you hurt anywhere?" I asked.

She turned and raised her knees. "Bruised ankles," she said.

"Anything else?" Fred said.

"I don't think so. You guys are saviors. I'll never forget you as long as I live."

She started to cry softly, then stopped.

"Next time," Fred said, "Make your pack light. Whatever's in there almost drowned you."

"It's my cook stove and cooking gear."

Fred shook his head.

"Do you need a ride?"

"No. I'm staying right here until I figure things out."

She sniffled hard and wiped the tears and creek water off her face.

"I am supposed to meet up with the trail crew in a little while. I was the smart one who'd been to this place before. I was the one who knew all the trails. Oh, little smart me."

She sniffled and cried once more, then wiped her nose, her face and said, looking into my face, "Do I look all right? Am I still OK?"

"You look lovely," I said.

"Well, let's not fall in love on the river bank," Fred said, chuckling. "We have to get going."

Her eyes widened. "Do you really? Oh, I'm so sorry I messed you up."

"You didn't," Fred said, smiling. "We just stopped by to save your life."

She started crying again and I gave her a big hug.

"What is your name?" I asked.

"Sadie."

Fred said, "Well, Sadie, have a great life."

"Thanks to the both of you," she said.

We could already see her friends trundling down the white dusty road to the creek.

Chapter Ten

Who knows why things happen the way they do?

A friend of mine used to say, "The Shadow do."

As I write this, I feel my whole life revolving in a star-wheel of mysterious events. It is as if I am not myself. Rather I am the characters I write about. And all of those characters are real people.

Fred, my grade school companion.

Sadie, someone with whom I am now bonded for life.

Laura, my wife of twenty years.

Will Channing, with whom I may have a connection that goes back to the 17th century when each of our families knew each other.

Jay, my mystic Navajo mentor of twenty years.

It is so complicated a web.

Am I the spider of it?

I sit here typing and wondering because I am on a wooden banco in this old haunted adobe house. Below my butt is a wooden lid—the banco lifts up to reveal a secret book locker into which I have placed some of my most precious books.

To return to the spiderlings, the web of tracery that ties us all to one another…I refer again to the book locker. It's guarded by a family of black widows.

I am not making this up. It's true. These are spiders I have always had an affection for. Once bitten twice shy? No, the opposite. Once bitten, forever tie.

I am bound to these dangerous spiders in the same way that Spider-man is in the comic and film. I was bitten by a black widow and it took months to heal and I still have the scar on my right thigh more than sixty years old. I can still feel it, and often do, to remind me of the connection.

We are connected to everything which is why we call it the web of life.

These selfsame spiders have followed me from one place to another. It is hard to believe but true. In every house where I have lived these spiders turn up. Once I was typing a novel and my bare feet tickled what I thought was a piece of material under the desk. Turned out it was a black widow web. I had been touching it with my big toe for over 35,000 words and for about 100 hours and until we moved from that house on the sand, the widow family was always there. What a tangled web we weave...

And the widows seemed to have followed me to our present house as well, for they are right under, I have to say, my ass.

I like to think they are writing this.

When I returned from Clear Creek, I met Laura with open arms and a full minute hug and she said, "Why the gloves?"

I explained. She said, "Will you ever be normal?"

I shook my head.

After I told her the whole story, including Sadie, she commented: "Did the coati hands save the girl?"

I nodded. "I believe so."

"Are you going to shave or wax that fur off? I mean, it may be cool to have coati powers but you have to face the day with hairy hands that look, well, more than a little strange."

"That's where the gloves come in."

She gave me a green-eyed stare. "You mean I have to get used to them."

"The gloves and the hands. I will just be patient and wait for Al-lan to return and tell me what to do. He got me into this, and while it's kind of cool, it's also kind of scary. I wake up in the night, see my hands and want to scream."

"Well, maybe it will help you make some money." She chuckled.

I said, "Freak show?"

We both laughed.

"I admit," Laura added, "that something very funny is going on in this cosmos of ours. Like, take last week, while you were gone. A woman calls from a magazine in Florida saying they would like to hire you to write weird op-ed pieces about humans that are part animal. I know it sounds weird, but no weirder than coati fur paws on my husband. Actually, it all seems quite normal for an abnormal person such as yourself."

"What are they paying?"

"Get ready for this."

"OK, I'm almost ready. Now!"

"They'll pay you enough to live, well, rather comfortably."

"And I thought no one was reading any more."

She gave me her wary, weary sidelong look. "They're not."

"Then why would they waste their money?"

"They're not."

"Be specific please…"

"So, it's like this, they want you to write the stories and they put them in their magazine. After that they may do audios. They will also be published in Canada and the UK. I think the editor said the BBC wants a piece of this, too."

I sighed, knowing there was a catch.

She saw it in my eyes. "You need to be based in Florida, at least for the first part of the assignment, then they want you to live in Jamaica. They are even giving you a laptop as a bonus for working for them. You know how expensive those things are…"

"I will still need a fax machine to send my stories. You know how bad the communication system is in the Caribbean."

"They'll probably send one of those over, too."

"So, the catch is…"

"A guy named Mr M is running the magazine."
"Like M in James Bond. Cool."
"He's obviously very wealthy."

Chapter Eleven

The first thing I had to do was shave my hands, or rather, hand claws. I also had to do a good manicure, a filing, of said claws. But removing the hair was a chore. At first, I shaved them the same way I shaved my face. But the coati fur grew back fast and, worst of all, seemed to thicken. I was beginning to feel like a spider, my hands scaring me every morning when I woke up.

Laura came to my rescue. "Why don't I wax those paws of yours," she offered.

I took her up on it. It hurt like hell. "How do women do this?" I asked her when she was in the middle of a hair removal exercise.

"Well," she said with a little half-laugh, "most women don't have this much hair to get rid of."

Without going into more details, suffice to say, a good waxing worked. After which I wore what they call "sun gloves". Soft cotton driving gloves that come up to the knuckles, sort of like stockings, to prevent sensitive skin from getting too much UV rays.

Most of the time I tried not to look at my hands. But the one good thing was that as the hair grew, so did the musculature. I surprised myself by removing beer tops with one turn. One day without meaning to I punched a hole in a can of tomatoes with my thumbnail. After that I cut the nails clean to the quick. I hesitated to wonder what I'd be like in a bar fight.

The magazine had the misleading title of *Aquamaze,* which sounds like an aquatic mag when the subject matter was scientific. Anything to do with the largest planetary liquid on earth. Was I the oddball item? The mystic scientist?

Where did I fit in exactly?

I didn't. Yet.

They definitely wanted someone who could write weird stuff that was true. I was pretty good at doing that. In short order, I was given air travel to Florida, to Marco Island, to be exact. There, in the midst of heat, humidity, muggy, buggy somewhat-lovely subtropics, I met with Mr Len Coppard, the senior editor of *Aquamaze* I sort of knew him. He was once the acquisition editor at *Skywriting*, the Air Jamaica flight magazine that published some of my Caribbean ghost stories.

He was small, bald, quick-to-smile, curious, inflexible, big eyed, and uneasy around people. I could sense that right away, but he gave me the good news first. One of his board members had secured my salary for one year.

"What subjects do you want me to tackle first?" I asked over coffee and Cuban pastry. We were in his office which overlooked Marco's silky sand beach.

"I want you to write," he said, "whatever you please. Mr M has given you that option."

He let that settle for a moment.

"So, according to your email memo, you reserve a space each month for my piece."

"Column," he corrected.

"Number of words?"

He drank his coffee down with a single gulp, like it was a shot.

"Anywhere from 1,000 to 2500."

He stared at me with his uniquely compassionate, teddy bear eyes. The eyes belied the iron will of a real grizzly, I supposed. I'd never had an editor that let me get away with a piece of writing that short and paid me to do it. Paid me well. No, very well.

"Is this for real?" I asked. I laughed to show him I meant no disrespect.

He stared at me for a second. The teddy eyes hardened.

"Would we fly you down here for a joke?"

My turn to stare at him while I thought of an answer.

Oddly, I couldn't come up with one. But at last I said, "You pay me for a year to write anything I want and it's one monthly article every issue plus you let me pick my subject?"

"Yup." He grinned for a nanosecond.

"So when do I start?" I smiled. This was going to be fun. Maybe more fun than I'd ever had as a writer.

He poured a full cup of coffee from the silver carafe, and downed it as before. Then he said, "Oh, sorry" and poured me one. The coffee was very strong and very high quality just like his well-appointed office. It even looked like he had a real ceramic Picasso behind his long tropical mahogany desk.

"That looks like a Picasso," I offered.

"That's because it is."

"How does one get a job like this?" I asked, sipping my coffee and eating a guava pastry.

He chuckled for the first time. "One," he said, underscoring the word with sarcasm, "has to not write like that." Then he broke into a surprising guffaw.

I got a sudden chill, and said "I mean, quite honestly, I've mostly written for moderate magazines with small budgets. I am what you might call a B-list writer, a good one but not a very rich one if you know what I mean."

"We pay well," he said in a neutral voice.

I had to ask…"Why me?"

"Your lucky number came up."

"How come?"

"It's very simple," he replied. "Mr M read a novel you wrote called *The Evil Chasing Way*. He liked it. No, that isn't quite right. He found it fascinating. He read it several times, I am told. Then he phoned me and said, "Hire this guy. That's all he said, but I assumed he wanted you to write for us, not polish desks or empty trash." He smiled and made a sort of funny clicking noise, from which I knew his teeth were false.

He waited while I digested the impossibility of my new job. "Is Florida to be my base of operations?"

"Heavens no," he said with a mild scowl. "You'll be based, as I said, in the Caribbean. It's *Aquamaze*, you know."

"Florida has tons of water wherever you look."

"Florida's got boring water."

"I see what you mean." I stared through his office window at the vast expanse of beach, which at 10:30 in the morning, glinted and almost glowed so emptily that it seemed to resist description. Beach boredom, it said.

"I get it. You want—"

"We want the exceptional. Period."

"You want wacko, you want weirdo, you want impossible to believe."

"Yup."

"Can you ship me a fax machine? I'm going to need it because the signals in Jamaica are unreliable."

"No problem. We're also giving you a laptop, too."

So I was off to the races. We shook hands and I walked out into the air-conditioned nightmare of Florida's sun and sand paradise.

Chapter Twelve

I began to plan my escape from Florida even before I entered the patio bar at the Hotel Iglesia.

One Irish red ale later, I eased into my cushioned chair and breathed deeply. The salt air tasted sweet. It was getting on past 8 PM and here I was—a writer formerly out of work, now on a busman's holiday. No, a junkman's obligato. No, again. I was employed. Suddenly I felt the quickening heartbeat of a writer on deadline. This was a monthly I was writing for but now they wanted me to write an article a week.

As I was enjoying the bitters, the second tall glass of red ale, I stared at the lowering sun and realized how off-kilter I was. I glanced at my cotton-gloved hands. I looked like an out of work musician with sun paranoia.

The sun lowered at exactly the same rate as my ale glass. I could actually see the amber sun through the ale-tinted glass. An attractive woman tasting a martini to my left seemed, as I imagined, to be looking at my gloves. I smiled at her. "Golfer's itch," I said.

"Really? There's such a thing?" she asked.

"The doc says."

She looked away swiftly, as if she might catch it in the tepid Marco Island air.

End of conversation.

I wondered what Laura was up to, so I called her.

"Well," she said, "did you get it?"

"I always had it."

"Is it as good as it looked?"

"Better. When are you coming down?"

"To Florida?"

"No, to Jamaica. I'm a Caribbean correspondent."

I could actually feel the thrill of saying this. A real job in the Caribbean. I would write and post bizarre events from any place, any port of call in the West Indies. I was suddenly delirious. The ale? The heat? The beach? I hadn't looked forward to Florida at all. But now I was in love with it.

Laura understood. "When you get to Jamaica, call me. By then I will have found a house sitter in Tesuque. I've interviewed three so far. You know I think your old friend Will Channing may do it. He and his family."

I signed off and continued to commune with the sun. It was now an ale glass inch from the purple sea. Night would soon be upon us. I nodded just once at the barmaid and she brought me another red. No sooner did it arrive than the last sip of the last ale disappeared almost symphonically down my throat.

The sun was now edging into the waterline. Sun and sea had met. The convergence, for some reason, gave me a little chill.

Then it happened.

The entire length of the sea fire horizon turned green. It was the whip of a dragon's tail, the flash. Then the tail lashed again and the line of demarcation changed from dragon tail green to light purple and gold, and from this unreasonable color to frost-bitten plum.

There were now quite a few people on the beach, all of them making noises of astonishment, joy, even ecstasy. I heard sighs all around me. Warbles from a few women. Whistles and shouts from delusional men, as if that would make it come back.

A few feet away from me I heard a guy in red Bermuda shorts say, "First time for everything!"

"First time—for what?" the woman next to him said.

"The green flash," Bermuda boy answered.

So that was it.

I'd read about it for years. Now I'd seen it. No mistake about that.

An island wind crept up, as if it too were seeking the flash.

The sky darkened. Stars peeked through holes in the fabric of night.

I sat content in the darkness and then waiters came out and lit the fluted table lamps.

I remained still for a while, savoring the sweet shock of the moment.

There were writers who claimed the green flash altered consciousness. Be still when you see it, they advised.

So I sat as still as a toad.

The wind picked up and snuffed some of the fluttering lamps.

All around me people were still mumbling about the flash.

I heard a woman weeping at a table nearby.

A family with children was having a hard time keeping the kids in line. They wanted to get into the water and splash around. The father said, "No, silly, not barks, SHARKS."

I sat and looked at my cotton-covered hands. I felt like OJ Simpson when he put on the incriminatory gloves at trial. He held his hands at an angle and looked at them as if they weren't his but someone else's.

I laughed at this silly conceit.

Then whispered to myself—I could crush OJ like the old fogie that he is. I could break his fingers like icicles and throw the icy glass shards in his face.

Where in hell did that come from? I shivered in the shoulders.

I calmed myself down. "You're all right. Just breathe."

The Tibetan meditation requires left cupped hand to be covered from below by the right hand. Now, breathe deeply. Slowly. Count 16 breaths in. Count 20 breaths out. Repeat, and repeat. Until breathing becomes natural and normal and there is no counting. I felt inside my left top pocket where I often kept my fishing lures. The small medicine bag with the sacred feathers were there. I continued my deep breathing.

I opened my eyes.

I had fallen asleep.

In my dream the green dragon swallowed me.

I yawned, blinked.

My fourth beer was untouched. I downed it in a long, delicious syncopated swallow and wiped my mouth with the back of my cotton-gloved right hand.

The beer was flat but still a little tickly. Warm foam laced the inner curve of the tall glass. It was very dark. The people had gone off to bed. The bar was lit but nobody was there.

I got up and went inside the hotel. The lighting seemed insanely bright. I slowly ascended the carpeted stairs to room 68 on the second floor. One step at a time. It was reassuring in its own way. Like the slow Asian breath units, one and then another.

I was fast asleep by the time the green dragon tiptoed into my dreams.

Chapter Thirteen

In the morning the concierge called to say there was an envelope, some flowers and a complimentary breakfast waiting for me. Moments later the breakfast arrived. The flowers were an assortment of red and pink hibiscus with a white card signed by Len Coppard: "First day on the job. M wants you to write something intangible about the green flash. Good luck and have a nice flight. Due date for this 1500 word piece: On arrival or thereabouts. We already FedExed your fax machine. They should have it at Blue Harbour before 11:00 tomorrow."

He was spot on. No messing around for him. My plane was leaving at 2:00. The article was due tomorrow at 11:00, and I was feeling like a character in Dr. No at 9:00.

Breakfast: cheese grits, scrambled eggs, hot coffee.

On my way…

And my story was already writing itself.

The Flash, I decided, was another narcotic.

It drugged you and drained you and dragged you into fantasyland.

I dreamed of dragons.

Aside from the otherworldly colors of the Flash, I remembered something else. The air during the color shift was perfumed with something sweet. But what? Fresh sliced melons, maybe. Confederate Jasmine?

Not quite it.

The dragons were another story. They were like mountains that moved. They had eyes like cities in the night. They lapped at me like sea water. Their jade scales were slippery.

I began to write rapidly about the Flash. The sensations it tripped into my brain. A dragon smell came to me as I wrote, a waft of the spell-inducing datura that I'd sniffed at Clear Creek.

Datura…also known as devil's trumpet, moonflower, jimsonweed, hell's bells and thornapple. The innocent moth-flower that bewitched the unwary.

Had the Flash awakened the datura dream of weeks past?

I began to see that the experience of the Flash was more than a little puzzling. It was mind-altering. Just like datura. Or was it that the datura slept in my subconscious and could be triggered again by a visual image of mystic magnitude. Something like the Flash.

I lost myself in speculation and typed a manic tale on my laptop. A ferris wheel of altered states. The dragons, too, became a dreamlike part of it. They had cavernous bellies like Carlsbad Caverns.

I'd been there once and when they shut off the lights and the sudden absence of gravity made you lose your balance.

The dragons were like that once you were inside their luminous bellies.

I wrote: "In the belly of the dragon you dream deeply. You have no gravity. You swim effortlessly in a cavernous world of dragon-time. People swim past you like tropical fish. You know them, you recognize them. They are dead people you knew when they were alive.

I typed a series of sensations that fluttered across the screen of my mind.

What had happened to me after viewing the Flash was akin to being on acid. The Flash knocked me out. Then pulled me into the cave of my unconscious. As I lay immobile, unable to move, the Flash tantalized me with images from my past and my future.

I read what I'd written, expunged the typos, and walked to the front desk and asked them to fax to *Aquamaze*.

Coppard phoned me ten minutes later.

"Ah," he said, "magic. Terrific. Now let's see if M likes it."

I showered, shaved, gargled and gulped some more black coffee, ate a piece of mango, a banana, and glanced at my hands.

A little work needed to be done. I lightly passed the razor over them and pulled on my sun gloves. I put on my favorite flowery Bob Marley shirt where he is kissing a spliff. No shorts for me. Jamaicans respected trousers, as they called them. Dark blue creased trousers. The Bob shirt would've broadcast either old hippie, goofy tourist or bullseye target—or maybe of the above. Except that this limited edition shirt was one of a kind. It was designed by Bob's daughter, Cedella, and given to me as a gift. There weren't any like it. Jamaicans miss nothing.

I was on my way, or so I thought. I had about an hour before take-off.

Len called again. "M likes the story. "But he wants you to say a little more about the dragons."

Without hesitation, I typed *Aftermath of Dragon Flash*.

My eyes grow blacker by the minute.
I am looking inside myself.
I focus on the fur sinews of my hands.
The dragon is eating green plankton.
It falls like wet crepe and lands softly on my shoulders.
The dragon curls up, wraps tail, closes giant, city-size lantern eyes.
The cavern grows dark.
Now I am swimming in the bitter salty brine of the dragon's belly.
I pop out of its green skin.
I am a bubble of white dragon sweat.
I pop.

Two hours later I am flying over the Emeralds of the Queen Islands just off the Cuban coast and nearing the South Coast of Jamaica.

I wondered if M liked the poem. Maybe I blew it. But how could that be? The whole thing was so farfetched I could hardly believe it myself, and yet it happened to me. I wasn't seeing the film, I was in it. No, I was it. I'd have to wait for the fax from *Aquamaze*.

Moments after landing at Montego Bay, I got a courtesy call at the airport.

It was Len. "Says he loves your writing. Keep tripping."

Chapter Fourteen

Before leaving Marco, I'd stashed a fat amount of cash into my cowboy boots. Illegal as hell but banking in Jamaica is a form of nineteenth century colonial madness. The Queen still rules in the currency department.

Being arrested for cowboy boot banking might send me to Gun Court prison, but there was also the possibility I'd slip through the cracks in my Bob Marley signature edition of one shirt and my rodeo worthy boots.

I might be seen as some kind of crazy country singer. Besides Mick Jagger was living in Ocho Rios and other rockers were often in and out of the land of the Doctorbird. They always said, "Jamaica no easy". But, in reality, Jamaica was always easier than the U.S. of A. Any Caribbean island was—except for the banking.

As it was, long story short, they patted me down and let me walk through Customs with a wad of cash stuffed into my cowboy boots. My Santa Fe brother, Will Channing, was right. "I wore my cowboy boots through Tortola customs once with a couple of hundred thousand dollars crammed into my cowboy boots."

"Why?" I asked.

"I was buying a house. Needless to say, cash has instant purchase power. Checks take forever to clear. It's the way they do things, you know, 'easy in the islands' is actually a joke."

I believed him and now I believed him even more. The customs agents in Mo Bay were light on me. The boots were eyed with honor as was the shirt. I then got a cab to Ocho Rios or Ochy as my driver said.

Once out on the Main with my bags I was immediately accosted by a chisel-faced man who said in a whispery voice, "Want something fi sniff?"

"No, I'm good."

He persisted. "Want something fi smoke?"

"I have plenty of that."

He looked at my Marley shirt, glanced at the fancy boots and believed me.

"Want something naked fi play wid?"

"I don't like snakes."

"No mon, Woman!"

"Got one at home."

He shook his dreadlocks. "What you want is *shrooms*."

"I have some nice rooms waiting for me."

He grimaced. "Mushrooms, mon."

I exhaled, shook my head. The sun was getting to me.

"Don't need it, I've got enough problems."

He stared at me in the sun-stunned, narrow street as the myriad old and new cars were honking and higglers were bonking their carts, and the hustling on all sides of me was giving me a headache.

The street dealer's face formed a dark question mark. "You muss need sumting, mon."

"I've got enough problems," I said wearily.

"You don't even know what problems is," he snapped, and walked away.

He was right.

I watched him weave through the crowd of people.

I breathed deeply. The exhaust fumes were thicker than thieves. They blunted the sun and lay heavily on the little mountainside city. Somewhere up in those climes of waterfalls, happy lizards and burnished white clifftop dwellings Jagger was twiddling his toes.

But I wasn't being paid to chase mystifying old rockers who wouldn't and couldn't die, not here anyway. I was being paid, as my boots could testify, to write stories of Castenadian charm. Stories to baffle precise minds that were bored with their own precision.

It was about then that the most amazing man I've ever met, met me.

He introduced himself. "My name is Mackie."

How he found me is another story.

Chapter Fifteen

His face was dark teak.

His white teeth the color of new snow.

His voice a low rumble.

He spoke only in short, truncated patois.

"How'd you know it was me?" I asked.

He smiled.

"Mike told me you a-come."

"Michael Gleeson, owner of Blue Harbour?"

"Yah, mon, Mike."

"I just got here. How did you know me."

Mackie laughed.

"Me see you before me see you."

"Mike show you a photograph?"

"No, mon. Me see you in a vision."

"You mean a dream?"

"Youth dem call it dream. Old mon seh vision."

He took me to Burger King on Main Street.

"I don't usually eat this stuff," I told Mackie.

He nodded. "All a you eat french fry."

He was right. I would, and did.

While we sat at a clean table and I nibbled fries in the extremely cold AC, I watched a *beggarmon*, as they say, digging in a dumpster, looking for something to eat. "I have a problem with that," I said.

"No problem," Mackie said.

"I mean, I find it hard to eat when there's someone who has nothing to eat."

Mackie said nothing.

I had a pocketful of "smalls". Jamaican ones, twos and fives. I got up and walked out into the heat and put a hand on the man rifling through the trash. He had laid out selections on a wax paper. Half-eaten food. Some scavenging, silver-eyed blackbirds hopped around him, pecking at each other, spoiling for a fight. The dumpster hunter didn't see them, nor did he seem to see me, as I handed him a handful of smalls. These he brushed out of his way along with my hand. But he never looked up from his trash binge search. He wore rags, mere fringes of clothes. His eyes were red. He had no teeth.

I spoke to him in patois.

I said, "Hey, mon me haff some money fi you."

I pushed the smalls into his hand.

He looked at them. His face was expressionless. It said, "What is this?" But his mouth never moved. Nor did he look at me.

Then he squashed the money into a ball and dropped it into the dumpster.

I walked back inside, shaking my head.

Mackie was smiling. "Dem no deal wid that."

"Beggars don't deal with dollars?"

Mackie's grin widened. "No, mon." Then he added, "Mon so deep inna Babylon him see nuttin but him own hunger."

He shook his head, "Same way Babylon eat up the world."

Outside in the white hot sun the broken man laid out burger-and-bun while the blackbirds stabbed at portions that dropped from his mouth to the pavement.

"Oonoo must eat," Mackie said, his voice rumbling.

I knew my patois but I didn't know that word.

"Oonoo?" I asked. "What does that mean?"

"In Africa it mean, all of you."

A little later, he drove me in a rented van to Blue Harbour, the 1940s funky hotel on the rocky cliffs of Castle Garden. The old stone building had once been the home of playwright-actor-singer, Noel Coward. The faded white, two-story main house was built into the sea facing hillside. The surroundings were creeping and dripping with tropical flowers, almond trees, Panama tall palms, hibiscus and aurelia bushes.

Mackie dropped me off at the kitchen where a friendly woman named Pansy explained that I would be staying upstairs "Where Mr Coward used to stay."

Even though I'd lived off and on in the Caribbean, I was undergoing a bit of culture shock.

Len Coppard had booked me in an informal guest hotel where Laura and I had stayed once before many years ago. The atmosphere reeked of romantic, literary bygone days. Edwardian books lined the shelves, the pandana plants hugged the margins of every wall, John Crow buzzards made long lazy sweeps through the green avenues of almonds. It was a dream. I smoked a small spliff and lay down on Mr Coward's upstairs four-poster and wondered again how I'd gotten the lucky ticket.

To paradise?

Or a pretty version of Hades?

Was it a tropic-layered Babylon, no worse, no better than Florida?

A place of many hungers?

Had the green flash followed me?

Was I in the belly of the dragon?

Or was I just a stranger in a strange land, destined to gift broken-down beggars fishing through the trash?

I slept. I dreamed.

Mr Coward materialized, sun-browned, white towel around waist, Rothman cigarette bobbing in a refined, handsome mouth.

Chapter Sixteen

The dream smoke went deep into my unconscious. I awoke with a start, sat up, looked around. The sun was sinking. Blue Harbour was aglow in the spoor of wine-colored light. I felt dry mouthed and dizzy. I'd slipped my sun gloves off before I nodded off. My hands were exposed. Hairy and offensive, to me, even though I was used to them. Still, to my eye, the tapers of my fingers were more animal than human. They were gross and I knew it.

I breathed deeply of the salty air.

Then came an electric shock.

Someone was squatting in the shadow of the tall seaman's chest in the west corner of the room.

I did a double take.

Mackie.

He appeared blue in shadow. The sun was down. Darkness filled the antique room. The tiny frogs that sing from the trees were starting up and with them the orchestral cries of the croaker lizards. More crash than cry, they sounded like rocks being banged together.

I yawned, my eyes on Mackie, whose eyes were on my hands.

"Wha' appen?" he questioned, nodding at my weirdness.

"I can't explain it," I said.

"Obeah mon put him spell on you?"

"Maybe."

He didn't move or say anything."

I yawned again. "Some herb," I said.

"Yah mon."

Somehow his bass voice gave me confidence. Like a guardian of the night.

"I wanted to make sure you were all right," he said in pure English. He switched back and forth. "Duppy 'ere, y'know." Pure patois.

"That's what I've been told. De duppy dem."

"Yah mon. Whole heap of ghost in dis here place. Dem love ruin."

"They love to ruin things?"

"No mon." He smiled. "Me seh dem love haunt and ruin, heartbreak place like Blue Harbour." Then he lit a cigarette, blew some deep blue smoke that curled in the sea wind. The ember of his cigarette brightened as he drew on it, then faded. "You speak patois?" he asked.

"Sometimes."

"How long?"

"How long do I converse in it, you mean? Or how long have I been speaking it?"

"How many year, me seh."

"Since 1968 when I first came to the islands."

"Y'know, Jack—all right if I call you that? —we don't really call them islands. We call them nations. Islands comes from all that colonial business."

I replied, "OK, Mackie, call me Jack, that's what they call me in the other nations of the Caribbean. Truth is, I get that. Nations versus islands. And you can speak any way you like to me, but I'd rather the patois, it's such a beautiful language."

"Yah, mon, it made up of French, Irish, Scottish, English, Spanish and African. Maybe even a little Jewish mix in, too. Dem come from Spain, the Jews. Dem call dem Portugals long ago cause dem no want Jews."

He drew on his cigarette, exhaling through his nose.

Then he asked a strange question. "You ever meet the Magistrate of the Queen?"

I hesitated, and my brow must've wrinkled. "Odd question, Mackie."

"Well, him come here soon. Mr Scott."

"Who is he and why would he come here this late in the day?"

"Him own Blue Harbour. Him check every now and again."

"I thought Mike Gleeson owned Blue Harbour."

"Mr Coward sell the place. Or him buddy do. Mr Scott buy Blue Harbour with Mike and Michele, him wife."

I nodded. "And you say he's coming here tonight?"

Mackie said, "True. Him come in one hour. Mr Scott, now, him speak English like a lord. Him see himself as a high upper class mon."

"Mackie, I'm a little nervous about this. I just got here and now this Mr Scott is coming here I am still stoned from one spliff and seeing the ghost of Mr Coward and…"

"No problem."

He eyed me. He was a shadow, but I could see his eyes twinkling. He thought it was funny.

"Mek you put on your glove dem," he warned. "Mr Scott nuh like obeah business."

Chapter Seventeen

"The problem, Mackie, is that I'm feeling a bit hazy in the head."

He gave me that deep gravelly laugh of his.

"Follow me," he said.

We walked on the rain wet walkways downhill, then cut across into the jungle where there were no pathways. It had rained while I slept. The fan palms tickled with raindrops. The pandana bushes grabbed at the ankles. Sometimes, looking down and watching where I put my feet, I walked into a hibiscus bush. It was not quite dark-night but veils of darkness were coming one shadow at a time.

Then, suddenly, we stepped clear of tangle and stood on a precipice of reef rock 30 feet above the crashing waves.

Mackie had weaved his way through the ramparts of greenery. I had forced my way through the bush and was now soaking wet. But Mackie was dry as a bone. His yellow knit shirt as fine looking as ever. His well-creased trousers sharp and neat. It was as if he'd transported himself through the air instead of a tropical rainforest.

He knelt down by a corner of the precipice.

In the last afterglow, reflected by the sea, I could see a small planted bush. One that had been carefully tended.

"Dis is bird pepper," Mackie remarked.

He snapped off one of the peppers and I saw that it was the size of my thumb and as red as red could be in the dimming light.

"Bite him," Mackie said.

I did that—took a bite of the pepper, chewed it fast and swallowed.

"I hope that wasn't a stupid thing to do," I said.

Mackie shook his head, very serious and said, "No mon."

Same time, a furnace was lit in my belly and I began to sweat from every pore. I sweated so much in so short a time, I couldn't see from the sweat that rushed down across my forehead and stung my eyes.

"I have to sit down," I said.

I raised my t-shirt and dabbed my eyes. Then pulled it off and wiped my whole face, neck and chest. The cooler air from the sea refreshed me. Presently I stopped sweating. My head was clear. The fog from the ganja was gone. But my mouth still burned as did my stomach.

I was stunned for a moment. The sleep stuffed person I'd been was gone. I now felt like an Olympian fresh from a winning run.

"What just happened?" I asked Mackie.

"Ready fi see Mr Scott?" he returned.

"I hope I don't scorch him with my breath."

He chuckled, "Let's go, I hear his limo idling."

We came out of the bush. From the other side of the hill. The side that faced the winding road and the terraced fields of pimento trees that led up to the second home of Noel Coward 1200 feet above the sea.

Mr Scott met us as we came down to the parking lot.

Mackie introduced me to Mr Scott and his driver who actually wore a chauffeur's cap. Mr Scott shook hands lightly, barely a graze. His hand was warm and soft-boned, as if it had never been met up with any hard work.

He had an aristocratic face. Even in the dark I could see the coin-like, old nobility of his features, the poetry and the intractability.

"I see you've already made yourself quite at home," he said as we entered the main house. The driver disappeared in the kitchen and came back with a pitcher of lemonade and three glasses. Mackie stood back, aloof.

Mr Scott's eyes fell to my gloved hands. "Doing a little polo with the horses?" he queried.

Gerald Hausman

"Now and then," I said. Then "Oh, you mean…I got a bad rope burn back in New Mexico. My doctor told me to keep them covered."

Mr Scott took a drink of lemonade. I could tell he knew I was lying. His eyes narrowed.

Mackie stepped up and said, "Actually we were harvesting some bird pepper together. Jack wore the gloves as protection."

"Was this after the rope burn?"

Now I knew why this man was the Queen's Magistrate.

He changed the subject. "So how do you find Jamaica, Mr Andrews. Is it to your liking?"

"What's not to like? This is the most beautiful country in the Caribbean. I'm delighted to be here."

"That's good to hear. Have you ever been to Barbados?"

"I've been to almost every island but Barbados. But I hear it's among the prettiest."

He looked hard at me. Then smiled. "Glad you think so. That is where I am from. But my roots, I have to say, are not in Africa. I come by way of Egypt."

"Ancient princes and kings," I added, respectfully.

This brought a genuine smile to his face. "If you think so."

Then he turned abruptly to Mackie. "Things going well at old Blue Harbour, Mackie?"

Mackie smiled. "No problem."

Mr Scott frowned. "I like that expression, Mackie, about as much as 'soon come' which in my book means 'never come' or rather…"

He glanced toward me and added, "It's when someone says he'll be right back and has no intention of doing so. It's a polite but convenient way of saying, 'bye bye' or rather, 'see you tomorrow or…possibly, never again.'"

No one laughed. But I could tell he didn't expect anyone to do so.

He turned his full gaze to Mackie.

"I wonder," he said, "how that wall safe is doing upstairs."

"Locked still," Mackie said.

"How inconvenient," Mr Scott said. He took another drink of the lemonade.

"More, Errol, please." Errol ducked forward, his hatted head bobbed in subservience, and he poured another round for all of us but Mackie who now stood at one remove, but farther back in the shadows than before.

"I say, Mackie, would you be kind enough to show us the inconvenient wall safe. I would like Jack to see how things run, or rather don't at old Blue Harbour."

Mackie moved at a good clip up the stairs to the second floor. We passed through the four-poster bedroom and walked into the hallway where there was a closet hidden from view by a surprising array of suits from the 1920s.

"Museum pieces of Sir Noel," Mr Scott said to me.

Mackie swept them aside. They slid awkwardly, scraping on their rusted and decrepit hangers. With the hall light brightly shining, I saw the safe: Armstrong & Rutger faded gold lettering across the front. Like the coat hangers, the safe was worn down by years of salt-attrition.

"So, here is the problem," Mackie grumbled. "This door won't open. When, and if, you open, it won't close. I kind of hammer on it. But it has a mind of its own and only admits entry when it feels like it."

"You mustn't hammer on things, Mackie. Let's see if the old combination works. If it does, you might put Mr Andrews' passport in here, but leave the door partly closed but not locked."

Mackie said, "Not possible."

Mr Scott replied, "It's a trick only I know about. When was it last breached, Mackie?"

"Breached…" Mackie answered with a laugh.

Mr Scott fiddled with the knob. His round back blocked our view. The combination clicked, and he forcefully plied the onyx lever that opened the door…

…and nothing happened.

Finally, after the fourth try, he turned to Mackie, then to me. Shrugging, he said, "No go, Mackie."

"Like me seh."

"As I said," Mr Scott corrected.

"Let me try," I offered.

Mr Scott looked skeptically into my eyes.

"Are you a safe cracker, Mr Andrews?"

"No, but I have strong hands."

"Before or after the rope burn?"

I smiled, stepped into position beside him. The closet smelled of mildew and outdated, time-worn theatrical clothing.

Mr Scott moved to one side. Then he made an open palm, be-my-guest gesture.

"Don't bother with the numbers, they are spot on," he told me.

My back was to him now, so I tugged off the glove on my right hand, placed my long linear coati fingers into the crusted crack of the safe door, and gave it a hard pry. One, then two. On the third try the safe wheezed open revealing a flashlight.

Amazingly, the flashlight was on. A beam of yellow light rested upon shelved papers, brownish folders with primeval elastic on them. There were also stacks of red, white and blue poker chips from some long gone game, and fat envelopes stained with paper clip rust.

I re-gloved, turned to Mr Scott and Mackie. "How could that be?" I asked.

Chapter Eighteen

After Mackie went home to Highgate, the town founded by Oliver Cromwell in the 17th century, Mr Scott, the Queen's Magistrate, was driven back down to Kingston.

I sat by myself on the second-floor veranda overlooking the windy crags of the North Coast.

My mouth was still buzzing from the bird pepper. But now I knew that if I got blitzed by Jamaican ganja I could always rely on Mackie's bird pepper to bring me down. There was a certain "mouth memory" of that voluminous heat. If you wanted to stir it up again all you had to do was wiggle your tongue around, and it would light up again.

So I sat on a Coward couch from the 1940s and thought about the rust-caked flashlight and its incendiary beam of secret light.

This triggered some thoughts about my next deadline.

It occurred to me I had a new story to write. The theory of relativity as applied to "the flashlight in the safe".

This was not Newton's apple. But rather Einstein's beam of light traveling across the universe.

I got my laptop and wrote *Sir Noel's Flash*.

It seemed to me that parallel take on life fit next to my last piece, *The Green Flash*.

I remembered Zen poet Philip Whalen telling me, "Your writing when you use image/experience/flash" is especially appealing to me. He went on about this and I could see in my head not only Whalen's great poem *Sourdough Mountain Lookout* but also Ferlinghetti's *Dog*. Ferlinghetti let the dog sort of write the poem as he wandered the streets of San Francisco. Where the dog went, and what he saw, was the poem. No wonder Ferlinghetti named that dog Homer.

So now I tripped the light fantastic with images conjured by an entrapped single beam of light. A light that shouldn't be there. A time-space-continuum beam that lasered through the cosmos. I wrote about Al-lan and his so-called "matrix of harmonic forces". A universe commanded by its own elegance. A new take on "Schrodinger's Cat".

I recalled Al-lan saying to me, "A woman, let us say, leaves a park bench at two in the afternoon and she goes back to her second story apartment and stays there for the rest of that day and night. But her friend, let's call him Harvey, sees her there on that bench at seven that evening. Is Harvey inventing the sighting? Is he making it up? No, the elegant universe requires that something of her essence is still there, and it is shaped the way she is in atoms of intricate light."

In my elliptical writer's brain I imagined Al-lan going further: "The essence of that essential lady is like your flashlight beam that remains lit in a locked safe for forty some years."

I continued my imaginative conversation with Al-lan. "So, a few years ago," I told him, "I walked in the Vicksburg cemetery where one of the worst sieges of the Civil War had taken place. And I swear to you I heard the gunshots at midnight, and felt the cannonballs ripping the earth. In the lull of battle I heard Confederates begging tobacco, and then the Yanks just took some over to their trench."

I could hear Al-lan laughing. "What you primitive earthlings call the time-space-continuum is nothing more than a flashlight beam in a locked safe."

"Time is etched on the fabric of the universe," he said.

When I finished writing the story for *Aquamaze*, the cold dew of a summer night in Vicksburg in 1978 had trickled down from 1865 and then it had dried in Jamaica in 1985...

A flashlight beam shut off in my head.

I saw empty night and the fog enshrouded streetlights on the long double bend of the road curving like light refraction all the way to Port Maria and on to Port Antonio.

Sound, too, curved in the crush of space and the trills of the tree frogs and the answering croaker lizards made a pulsation that fired my imagination all over again. I heard Agamemnon's trumpets far off in the Port Maria night. A street band? Probably.

And so, dreaming on Sir Noel's Edwardian couch, I drifted. The sun rose over the palm tops of Cabarita Island. Twenty-five feet below me, the wind rustled around the cottage once lived in by Hollywood starlets. Below that, in the sea itself, the pirate Blackbeard scraped whelks off a rock with his friend, Henry Morgan.

…A flashlight beam came on in my head.

And I was awake.

Chapter Nineteen

I had only been in Jamaica for a few days, but already I felt—in spite of the barrage of mysteries—at home.

I spent the morning after the safe cracking night correcting copy on the time/space piece, and sent it to Len at *Aquamaze*.

He sent me a positive message.

There was a peculiar postscript: "M says he saw you in Ocho Rios." What?

That stuck in my brain.

Mackie's answer to it was simple enough.

"We come and go."

"By that you mean Jamaica is a kind of portal for all things seen and unseen. Things that come and go."

He wouldn't speak further about it. I let it go. But not really. The man you worked for…the one who paid your way into the mysteries…was a duppy?

That thought turned into a hungry cockroach.

At the end of the day, Mackie, who came and went like a shadow, showed up in a pastel blue print shirt covered with blueprint drawings of white yachts. He wore his usual dark blue pressed pants and had a 1930s porkpie hat on his head. To say he looked jaunty would not do him justice.

"Have something for you," he said.

He handed me a small brown, almost furry fruit. "Naseberry," he said. "Spanish call them *sapodilla*".

It was a kind of scotch butter tasting grainy fruit. The flavor was maybe a combination of apple pie and cinnamon. Super sweet. Weird but kind of wonderful. The lingering aftertaste was like caramel. Something you might eat at a state fair somewhere.

"Not everybody like them," Mackie said.

"Good for what?" I asked, "aside from eating."

"Them make chewing gum from them."

"You want something fi write?"

"Naseberry?"

"No mon. Nine Night."

"What is that?"

"Nine Night like what them call Irish Wake."

"Ceremony of the dead."

"No mon. A ceremony of the living."

"…with the dead present."

"Yah mon. But him no dead."

"I don't understand."

"Follow me," he said.

***

Mackie moved swiftly. Like dark water. His strides were quick. I had to jog to keep up with him.

We crossed the double bend road that went to Ocho Rios and headed into the Blackwell hills of heavy shade pimento trees. Goats blatted at us. Pocket parrots chittered. An old brown cow mooed and gave us a melancholy stare.

The path narrowed, twisted. We were going up into deep bush at a forty-five-degree angle. Mackie picked up a pimento stick and thrashed at the tall grass that grew around our knees. Diamonds of dew scattered and landed like ice on my bare legs.

"Y'see the mon there?"

I stopped to get my breath.

"What mon?"

"They seh him have a yellow eye."

I shook my head.

"That mon see Marcus Garvey get stoned for a bowl full of rice."

We proceeded upward. The goat path grew steeper.

It came to me that a man had appeared to our left or our right and Mackie had seen him but I had not.

I knew, however, about the horrible stoning of Garvey. In the 1930s the Jamaican government, English to the core, paid people to hit Garvey with rocks while he gave a speech in the streets of Port Maria.

That speech, now famous, was about the Universal Negro Improvement Association. Garvey, founder of the Black Star Line, promoted the return of Africans to their ancestral lands. That much I knew.

"Where was that man you saw, Mackie?"

"Him sit on a stone in the grass."

"Near us?"

"Close by."

It seemed to me then that people could see *me* but I couldn't see *them*. Mackie laughed deep in his throat.

We continued on. While walking, pacing myself to keep up with him, I thought about the invisible man by the goat path. How old would he have to be, I wondered. In order to have seen Garvey in the 1920s?

Mackie heard me thinking. "That mon back there, him an old mon."

"How old do you think?"

"Hundred or more."

I knew people lived to biblical ages, the longevity of antiquity, in Jamaica.

I would have to find a way to meet this phantom and talk to him about Garvey. I chuckled to myself.

Was everything here phantomic and ephemeral?

Invisible until seen, and then not seen, in its entirety?

Was every little thing in this bygone backcountry made of particles that assembled, reassembled and disappeared?

After a while, we rested in a meadow where I glimpsed a man, flesh and blood person, covered in pimento ash. He was grey all over and looked like a rock man in a comic book I'd read as a kid—*Torak, Son Of Stone*.

We stopped and talked to him. The man was a charcoal maker, East Indian, by the look of him. The pungent smell of burning pimento wood and smoke-driven ash filled the small meadow.

What struck me though was the appearance of the cow. The same brown cow we'd seen 800 feet below when we entered the fields of Blackwell Hill. The cow looked not at Mackie or the East Indian charcoal maker, but at me. It chewed grass cud and stared into my face with great liquid brown-eyed familiarity. It gave me an eerie feeling.

It was as if it knew me.

We went on, ever upward until we reached the top of the mountain. We were now some 1200 feet above sea level. Blue Harbour glimmered against the blue Caribbean Sea of the North Coast.

We sat in new mown grass and watched a man scythe the brow of the hill with a razor-sharp machete. He bent down low and laid the grass low. Making me think of the Bob Marley song that was a different kind of bending.

"Bend down low, let me tell you what I know."

And there, off to the right, was that same brown cow looking into my eyes.

Chapter Twenty

We left the cow where it was standing.

The rest of that day we hung around Firefly Hill and the last house Sir Noel had lived in. Mackie was sitting, statuesque, at the end of the veranda that had once been the hideout of the pirate and governor, Henry Morgan.

As for me, I sat in the Firefly bar on the brow of the hill that looked out on the entire North Coast. I drank a couple of shandies—lemonade and Red Stripe beer. They went with the view.

Under my shirt, I felt the little feather-concealed paho-pouch given by Sungazer, the Navajo medicine man just before he died.

I recalled our final conversation…

"Do you know where that last feather is to be delivered?"

"The place of blue water?" I asked.

"Where the blue water is the color of turquoise."

Then he spoke of a man who lived on a tall rock, as he put it. He will take the feather, and return to you the source of all life. I will know of this, I will feel it."

I reached into the soft white deerskin pouch and felt the feather. It was sleeping on a bed of cornmeal and corn pollen.

My own life was somehow conjoined with this dream-like appointment with destiny.

I wondered if the man on the rock was Mackie.

Or maybe…

I stared at the green eyes of the barman. Brown face, green eyes.

One small, curled feather was green. The other was blue.

I sipped the shandy and stared across Sir Noel's lawn, which dropped off so that the green sward of grass met the cobalt Caribbean sea.

It all fit…like a glove…

I looked at my gloved hands, shook my head.

Who would believe it?

The man with the coati fur paws.

Which reminded me: they were growing furrier by the minute.

Was the green-eyed barman staring at them?

I was a storyteller trapped in a story not my own.

At the end of the smooth mahogany bar, Mackie sat stoically as usual.

I wished, in that moment, to be him. He had a family. He had worries of his own. But he kept them to himself and they didn't seem to bother him. He often talked about his children: Lorraine, Lorna, Junior, Jerome. I knew them by face and name. It was one of the first things Mackie did. Bring his kids down from Highgate where they lived to meet me. Somehow that was important to him.

My mind focused on Laura, my wife.

She would be in Jamaica in a couple of days.

That would make things only half-seen wholly seen. She was good at seeing.

I swallowed the rest of the shandy.

***

Four hours later, after wandering all over the estate we were walking down Firefly Hill to the little village of Grant's Town with its great water tower and after collecting gourdies that had fallen off a gourdy tree damaged by one of the hurricanes evening slowly crept across the old estate.

We made our way to the rear of the property. It was here that Miguel, Sir Noel's butler, had lived with the master for twenty some years.

Miguel had died on the day I arrived in Jamaica. Tonight, all the preparations were being set up for the Nine Night ritual.

In a certain way, the African ceremony of saying goodbye to the dead was more dramatic than an Irish wake. More of a drama with penitent actors who were both mourners and celebrants. The solemnity was different, too. I had read about it but had never seen it.

Mackie and I made our way to the tiny, white, one-room board house in the thickets of palm and aurelia.

I no longer wondered why I was there. Mackie said I was invited. Being the only guest at Blue Harbour, and Blue Harbour being the annex of Firefly, and Sir Noel being the ghost, the duppy, in attendance…well, you must understand, this wasn't America or even Ireland. It was Jamaica and deepest Africa combined.

We came to a firepit where family members and friends were crouched, Caribbean fashion. The aboriginal squat.

Everyone was smoking small cigars and drinking ganja tea. A great black pot was boiling over the fire, and as Mackie and I drew near, two china cups were given to us.

The tea changed everything.

Mackie called it "bushweed". Whatever it was, it was strong. I felt a warm glow wrap around my heart and spread all around my chest.

As we crouched with the others, I watched the children play an African ring game. Round flat dark stones were passed from hand to hand. The idea was that the stones must not stop their circular, rhythmic orbit. If one of the children dropped their stone, he or she got a hard, rap across the forehand. This was delivered by the person kneeling close by.

And so, round and round, while the children chanted:

> *"Bruck dem, one by one, gal and bwoy*
> *Bruck dem, two by two, gal and bwoy…"*

The circle game would continue with the accompanying chant until one of the players fumbled their stone, and so got a good hard smack. Ten players, ten stones, all moving with an intense mad tempo.

When one of the players goofed and got his hand "bruk", then that player was out. But the game continued right along. As the circle got smaller, the passing of the stone got faster. Until only the winner, the one-stone holder was left. As I sat, entranced watching and listening, I heard the song go like so:

"Finger mash, nuh cry, gal and bwoy,
memba, a play we deh play…"

"What a weird game," I said to Mackie.

He drank his tea, set the cup on his knee. "No mon, it natural, like your musical chair thing…only this African game very, very old."

"Everything comes around goes around," I mentioned.

Mackie said nothing.

After a little while, he commented, "Stone game is like a rough-tough teacher. Telling everyone to pay attention, and stay alert."

We watched as the game came together with more laughter, hand smacking and stone passing.

Finally, Sir Noel's house keeper, Imogene, the wife of the dead man, Miguel, came to us and whispered, "You may go in now."

I followed Mackie into the little white house. The tree frogs were trilling loudly now. Pulsing in the black and leafy night.

The house was lamplit. A kerosene scent hung in the air. We walked slowly by an open coffin, but there was nothing in it. The interior silk was shiny and empty.

Mackie nodded once toward the Victorian high-backed chair on one side of the room.

Miguel, the dead, sat in it, his legs stretched out comfortably.

His shoes shined, his eyes open.

Dead? Not hardly.

It was impossible not to believe that he was staring at you.

It was a mistake not to think he was alive.

Yet he was dead.

Miguel had a lit cigar clamped in his teeth and he seemed to be sucking on it because it was issuing blue smoke in small puffs and the ember brightened when he seemed to inhale. But no smoke came out of any orifice.

His ears were plugged with nutmeg nuts; two, one in each ear. You could see the nuts protruding like ancient African hearing aids.

I looked at his face, damp and shining in the kerosene glow.

Miguel's jaw was shut tight with a knotted piece of pandana string. That was the only thing that gave him an unalive look. Otherwise he looked, and seemed, fully alive.

Unconsciously, I nodded toward him.

His brown eyes gleamed, as if in appreciation.

I could not wait to get out into the cool air of Firefly hill. But the ganja held me, as it did Mackie who spoke not a word.

We stayed until the first rays of sun climbed upward into the tall cedar trees.

The time passed quickly.

It was morning.

We walked down through the Blackwell woods. Neither of us said a word.

I wondered if I should have given the little green feather to Miguel. Or the blue. The white one was for the sea, where it collided with the rocks on the beach.

I could have slipped it into Miguel's suit jacket. Other people had given him other things. Flowers, shells, cigarettes and a cigar or two.

Someone put a gold enamel Rotary pin in his open palm. A child placed a doctorbird's nest on his knees.

Something kept me from letting go of the feather.

At the bottom of the hill, facing Blue Harbour, we could hear the dawn sea crashing on the limestone cliffs. As we neared the cattle fence, I glanced over my shoulder. The great brown cow was standing there looking at me.

This time, stoned though I was, and weaving a bit, I made for the cow.

I heard Mackie chortle once.

In distant, mist-beshrouded Grant's Town, the roosters were crowing.

I walked up to the cow, looked into its great liquid eyes.

It smelled of sweetgrass.

"Who are you?" I asked.

"You don't know me?" it answered.

Chapter Twenty-One

It was that in-between time, the space between dusk and dawn. What the ancestral tribes called the "time of deception." When things you see are an illusion. And things you do not see are real.

A cow, a round-eyed, brown hide, cud-chewing animal had spoken to me in plain English.

Considering that I was still high from the half gallon of ganja tea I had been drinking for most of the night, I needn't have questioned my state of mind, so I didn't.

I walked toward the cow.

"You know who I am," it said.

And then I knew him.

No doubt, it had to be my old outer-dimensional friend, Al-lan.

"You're in a new skin," I suggested, still a little doubtful.

"I always wanted to be a cow," he replied calmly. "I thought though there'd be no percentage in it. But I found out, being bovine is really great."

"In what way?"

"Well, first, hardly anyone notices you. Second, when they do, they give you no credence for having any intelligence. So you're free to rove around the fields of wonder with nothing pressing upon you except getting back to the barn at night. Well, I will admit that can be a pain in the butt. So, how are you getting along, brother?"

I watched him for a moment. He was just a big ass cow. But hidden inside his head were the secrets of the universe. No wonder he liked being bovine. He could see all there was to see and yet be almost unseen. To top it off he could walk most anywhere because, after all this was back country Jamaica. Cows sometimes walked down main street.

"I'm getting along just fine," I told him, stroking his long, thick, smooth neck.

"You're so…sleek and warm," I said, approvingly.

"Yeah, well, sometimes you get lucky. I've seen so much in this borrowed body of smooth skin, as you say. I'll tell you in a minute about the flying saucers landing in White River just south of here. But how the hell did you get here?"

"The usual way, I flew in a jet plane."

Al-lan, the cow, looked blankly at me. He continued chewing his cud. Some green slime slavered off his chin. "Wipe that off for me, will you? There are things cows can't do, you know, because of their tri-cornered hooves."

"You probably want to know," I said as I wiped his stubble chin with a sheaf of fresh mown grass."

"Thanks," he said, "I hate that dribbly feeling. Mind if I eat the rest of that clover grass you just wiped me with?"

I handed it over to him and for a moment he had a Mark Twain mustache while he contentedly chewed, his jaw moving from side to side while making a variety of clicking sounds.

"So," he said, "you're doing what, exactly?"

"I'm writing articles for an aqua-based magazine. Speculative journalism. The magazine is mostly science-based. But I'm the wild hair, so to put it."

"Well, you are that," he added. "What are you writing right now?"

I bent down and grabbed another handful of clover grass and he kind of inhaled it, cow-style, drawing it into his mouth with upward, downward and sideways motions of his square, elongated jaws.

"I'm in the middle of a piece about a dissonant flashlight that holds a beam of light for more than forty years while locked inside a wall safe hidden in a closet."

Cows don't normally laugh—at least I didn't think they did—but I heard something of a chomp-and-a-chortle chuckle from him.

His great round, brown eyes watered a little, too.

"I hope you're telling them that it was the enemies of Xerxes that flipped the switch on that. They go immaterial. No outer skin at all. You can't see them."

"Who?"

"The Annexerian people. They've been trying desperately to locate me. It didn't occur to them to look into the mouth of a cow, so they're snooping around in an old safe, I guess. Not surprising though. Who knows what they might find."

"To what purpose?" I asked.

"That I couldn't tell you. But just like your people, they have a humanoid impulse to start wars and decimate populations."

"...and you are the fly in their ointment, I suppose."

"That is correct, sir."

"You are all about harmony and they are all about disharmony."

"Just so."

The light was beginning to turn the leaves to gold.

Morning was on us, leaf by leaf. Stem by stem.

Al-lan stopped his cud work and looked at me straight on. Which is to say, he looked at me sideways with one all-seeing eye.

"Would you like me to give you more story on that?" he asked. "Maybe you can use it in your article."

"Please," I said. "I'm stuck with no conclusion. The dissident flashlight needs to be somehow connected with Einstein's theory of relativity."

"That old saw," he scoffed, "$E=mc2$."

I nodded.

"OK," he began. Let's use music as our metaphor here. Follow me now, I'm going to talk fast, as I often do. So, in the circle of fifths, musically speaking, you have the thing called the flatted fifth. Also known as the Devil's Interval. It's a tritone note that gives you the chills."

"The ultimate dystopian sound," I suggested.

"That's it. Bob Dylan said it pretty good in his book *Chronicles*. Well, to be honest, I read before I had hooves, but that's beside the point. Dylan called this new way of doing chords an 'incantation code' that was mostly unused by musicians. By using thematic triplets, according to Dylan, you could make your song, your voice truly hypnotic. "I could hypnotize myself," he said… "I could explode like an ice cloud."

"That hits the nail on the head," I added. "since we're in an emerald steam cloud here in Jamaica. Go on, tell me more."

"Well," he went on, "Now's when I can relate it to the universe, as a whole, and you can use this in your article or whatever it is. You know what a black hole is?"

"An enormous gravitational field of darkness that sort of pulls things into itself."

"That's speculation, but good enough. In doing so, it may create amazing dissonance in the universal fabric of space."

"You mean kind of like a lesion in that fabric."

"Yes, a rip. Okay, now take me, for instance. I move through these wormholes in what you call outer space. Now, if a cosmic disturbance occurs I might get displaced for a while—"

"—until you find another suitable wormhole to travel through."

He swallowed his cud. "Another, please."

I gave it to him.

"So, anyway, when there's a lesion in a wormhole, it's like a child's ball when it starts to deflate. It could compress and destroy whatever's in it, oxygen in the child's ball, but absolute annihilation in the case of a wormhole."

"—And you've been in one of those situations, Al-lan?"

"Indubitably."

"How did you save yourself from being crushed into atomic particles?"

"You simply use Gorilla Glue."

"By that you mean some interplanetary substance that is, by definition, strong as a big ape."

He shook his head and for the first time I heard a bell ring.

Al-lan saw my surprise. "Yeah, yeah," he intoned. "The dumb farmer belled me up so I'd be just like the other cows. Of course, I couldn't talk to him about who I was and why a bell was a bit degrading, but anyway you understand, don't you, that I have used your commercial product, Gorilla Glue, to fix lesions in a wormhole in space."

I shook my head. "This is all a bit odd coming from a cow."

"It was easier when I was a dog?"

"Well, let's say, more familiar."

"Would you rather I be a praying mantis?"

Chapter Twenty-Two

The sun was well-risen now and people were on the double-bend road coming and going from Port Maria in one direction and Ocho Rios from the other, and I thought it best to terminate my desultory conversation with my friend from the planet Xerxes. He thought it best as well. "Put it all together," he said, "and the dissonant flashlight will make sense."

He continued, "The Annexerians were into that safe, like they're into everything else. They probably have a bead on you, my friend. Your article will annoy the hell out of them. Go ahead and rub them wrong. We'll get them in the end. They shit dissonance into the universe. We give them cow poo in return."

"By the way," he added, "I like your coati-fur fingers. "They're very becoming."

"Becoming what? I want to get rid of them."

"Patience, brother. You'll soon be missing them."

"You know that to be true, Al-lan?"

"Yes, very soon burning water will restore your human hands."

"Burning water," I mumbled. Another egregious, ultra-dissonant impossibility.

Then he ambled off and I remembered something he'd said a long time ago. "A cow's way of walking is a matter of math: it describes a hyperbolic paraboloid."

Everything possible was impossible, but only for a time. Just like impossibilities like Mt. Sneffels in Jules Vernes' novel *Journey to the Center of the Earth*. The other day I had been on Mt. Sneffels and it was in Santa Fe, New Mexico. I saw the sign and went up the mountain and breathed the thin, high octane air.

And now I was looking at a cow's butt at sea level.

I saw it now, his rear woggling, at a surprisingly precise angle, from left to right as he walked. You could follow it with a protractor. Pure Euclidian geometry. No question about it—a quadrilateral performance. Two pairs of parallel sides, hip bones, moving away from me. Ha,ha. A cow's geometric ass fading into gilded morning Jamaican dawn.

Euclid would be proud.

Math was in everything.

Even wormholes and Gorilla Glue.

But how to explain this stoned equation?

Al-lan always made sense when you were with him.

And I might add, especially when you were stoned.

But now I had to get back to Mackie, who, after sitting and meditating for a while, slipped through the Blackwell fence and went across the road to Blue Harbour.

When we met up moments later, he laughed.

"Talking to a cow," he said. "Ahhhh!" Gently he gave me a little push.

I laughed with him.

"Bob did seh all them things speak. Bird, animal. No reason you cyan't reason with a cow."

"You knew Bob, didn't you, Mackie?"

He leaned back, closed his eyes, and sang into the blue sky.

> *"Don't worry about a thing*
> *Cause every little thing*
> *Gonna be all right..."*

He sang in a raspy whisper voice just like Bob's only a little deeper, and the notes were right on, clear as the morning sun, and the timbre was just right and I got what Mackie meant, too.

A man can converse with birds and cows, and whatever, and Mackie told me, "Yah, mon. Me grow with Bob Marley inna St. Ann. Him know me grandmum who was a mystic woman."

"They call them *curandera* in New Mexico," I said.

He nodded. "True. Many name for same."

Then he asked me, "How you get that bloodfoot?"

"Bloodfoot?"

He pointed to my right foot.

"Oh, hell. I must've stepped on something. I don't feel it though. The ganja tea must've killed the pain."

"Dem put bruk glass bottom of fence. Sometime up top too when fence is made of cement. It keep the tief dem well away from the place."

"Well, I'm no thief but I catch a cut from the glass, that's for sure."

Looking at it while sitting, I saw a deep gash in the bottom of my foot.

Mackie told me to press the torn skin tight. "Me find Churchill."

I didn't know if that was a medicine or a man.

But the cut was deep, I could see that. And the tea was beginning to wear off.

This was going to lay me up for a while. Maybe more than a while.

Moments later, Mackie returned.

Churchill was a man.

Chapter Twenty-Three

Mackie introduced us. I was bleeding and Churchill, a man of few words like Mackie, began cleansing the gash in the arch of my foot. He opened the flap of torn skin, revealing a one-inch red hole.

"I am Winston Churchill. I live over in Albany."

"You live in Albany, New York?"

Churchill chuckled. "Albany, Jamaica. One hour from here."

"Is that near Friendship?"

"Not too far, not too close."

Then he said, "This is going to hurt."

I asked him, "Are you a doctor?"

He and Mackie both laughed.

They said, almost in unison, "Bush doctor."

Churchill's eyes crinkled at the corners. They sparkled. His fingers moved very fast. He scrubbed the wound from the inside with a wet cloth, then got me to lie down on the cold pavement under the standing pipe with my leg raised up.

The water hitting the wound full force was like ice.

"That hurt?" Churchill questioned.

He had one of the kindest faces I've ever seen. Now he applied pressure to the cut, which bled freely.

"Hurt?" he asked again.

I gritted my teeth. "I can deal with it."

"Now," he said, lowering the spigot handle and shutting off the water, "I will apply the lime and the salt."

I asked Churchill if he worked for the Thomas de Torquemada team.

His face showed no expression.

"Are you a professional torturer?" I asked, trying to make light of the situation by laughing.

"No, mon," he replied quietly. He had dark skin like Mackie, thin lips, magnetic eyes and healing hands.

Mackie smoked a small spliff rolled in brown cigarette paper. It was about a quarter of an inch long and he handed it to me. "You need this," he said gruffly.

I took a draw. The smoke was light, sweet.

A second later, I was easy in the islands.

Churchill pressed the halved lime into the wound, and squeezed.

The sudden sting made me sit up straight.

I gritted my teeth.

"That hurt?" Churchill asked.

I nodded.

Churchill smiled. "It natural, mon." He had beautiful teeth, short dreadlocks, and was like a copy of Mackie. Physically, they could have been brothers.

After the lime torture, Mackie went into the Blue Harbour kitchen. He came back with a bag of something. Churchill reached into the bag.

"That looks like sugar," I said.

"Table salt," Churchill told me.

Without a moment's hesitation, he poured a handful into the now bloodless cut, the flesh all white and soft from the lime, and held it there for a good long minute while I did some more teeth gritting.

When he was done with this phase of torture, he washed the wound with spigot water once again. After which he applied the final coup de grace—a green banana.

"What the hell?"

"This is the real cure, Jack," Mackie said. "The other just clean the wound."

It was a boil banana, as they say. The hard, green ones you see in the outdoor markets. Churchill opened it, splayed it with a gravity knife that shone in the sun. He threw away the inside, leaving only the raw skin,

"Now what?" I felt a bit woozy from the pain. But mainly from Mackie's tiny doobie.

Churchill said, "Me tie this to you foot bottom?"

I nodded. By now I was pretty well past the pain principle.

Surprisingly, I felt nothing I could name.

But after I thought about it, the green banana felt like something rubbery and wet. He tied it in place with a piece of string and told Mackie to get a clean woolen sock.

Mackie said, "Where your suitcase?"

I told him. He got one of my best cotton running socks.

Gently, Churchill eased it over the banana cure.

Then he and Mackie carried me like a wounded soldier up the veranda stairs and softly dropped me into Sir Noel's four-poster bed.

I closed my eyes and fell asleep.

In a dream I heard them talking. Churchill was saying, "Me don't think him need stiches."

"I saw you put your finger into that cut, maybe one whole inch, maybe likkle more."

"Most white bwoi no tek such pain."

"Him a different."

And then I drifted off and found myself in Jamaica in the long ago when a relation of mine got himself into the war of 1812. His ship sailed to Jamaica and I sailed with him in my dream of the bounding main. The salt spray stung his face and the tar from the cracks of the deck glued him in place and held him prisoner while the john crows came down to eat his heart.

I woke in a cold sweat in the middle of the night. I remembered my injured foot, but I couldn't feel it. There was nothing there but dark air.

Had Churchill amputated it?

I broke into a hot sweat. A fever dream.

I was thinking of my poor relative Ebenezer Fox and how he suffered from ship splinters during one of the sea battles, I came fully awake.

I was pinned to the deck of the good ship *Bream*. Sun-bitten, salt-eaten. The cannons were booming. The john crows were looming. I was a water dog, fresh for the picking. I was a boy of 13 years, a midshipman.

A face came close to mine. It was Obadiah Glasgow, the Portugal pirate who'd escaped the Spanish Inquisition. Like me, a misbegotten Jew, half English, half Spanish.

I woke again.

Shivering.

A teeth shattering chill iced my bones.

A dangling flashlight burned before my eyes.

Then a black nurse named Churchill in a starched white dress said, "Y'okay mon?" His eyes sparkled blue diamonds.

I fell into the ocean.

Sinking like a stone.

Deeper and deeper.

Into the layers of sargassum weed.

A paddle-wheeling cow churned by.

Its left eye winked at me.

The moon was in wicker shadow.

It winked in a sea wet harbor wind.

I felt my right leg.

It wasn't there.

I had no right leg.

Chapter Twenty-Four

Whatever happened was a miracle of bush medicine.

I'd heard about these things—cures of unaccountable beauty and mystery.

Healings medical doctors never dreamed of.

My entire right leg was asleep, but when I inspected my foot, the two-inch gash was a thin grey line. It looked like an incision made many years before. When I pressed the bottom of my foot where the shard of glass had torn my flesh, there was no pain nor discomfort.

When Mackie saw it, he let out one of his quick guffaws and said, "Green banana!"

I asked him if Churchill's gentle hand had anything to do with it.

Mackie replied, "These healers work like natural mystic. You know the song?"

Then he sang,

> "There's a natural mystic blowing through the air
> If you listen carefully now you will hear,
> Such a natural mystic…"

His voice trailed off.

Then, "Mi grandmother heal with eye, hand, boil banana, bush tea, snail shell, anything, mon, any ting at all."

He went on, "Old time healer used to draw on old African remedy. There was a myal woman, myal man, obeah woman, obeah man…all dem ting deh…in one same village."

He paused and nodded. "Yah, mon. All dem ting deh."

I went down to the kitchen and met my friends Pansy and Julie who were bustling about making a dish known as rundown. Also called "Rundun, fling me far, fling me for." Fresh caught mackerel, boil banana, "gratered" coconut. A bowl of cornmeal mush on the side with fried breadfruit. Three cups of Blue Mountain coffee, and I was ready to run up to Firefly, and I did. Running soft at first, then full-out, as Jamaican men appeared roadside and clapped hands when they saw me pumping up the hills.

Later I told Mackie, "Rundown mek me runup!"

In the afternoon I got word from Laura that she would be on a late night flight from Albuquerque coming into Mo Bay on Air Jamaica. Mackie got me a driver named Tall T who picked me up in his minibus called the Irie One. I learned that Tall T was also called Irie One. He had other names as well including Yellow due to his "high color" as they said. He was known as Uton, which was his given name. His school name, Ernie, was given to him because of the popular Jamaican singer Ernie Smith.

It was around sunset. Ernie drove down the main road through Race Course, and down to Oracabessa. There he stopped.

"Me tek you down to James Bond Beach," he said. "Then me show you the Jacob Ladder that change my life."

We made a stop and got out of the minibus. Many places in Jamaica had what was named the Jacob Ladder. A spiritual climb. Vines hanging off an eighty-foot cliff several of which dropped all the way to the golden sands of the beach.

"See the cliff? So, me faddeh him climb that sea cliff," Ernie said. "His two arm look like dis."

We got back in the bus and continued to drive.

As he drove he handed me his wallet. "See de picture deh?" There was a plastic window in the wallet and a very old faded picture of Ernie's father looked out at me. Ernie was right: the man was all arm. And his two arms hung down to his knees. No one could have such long arms, but this man surely did.

I handed the wallet back and Ernie then told the story. It went rambling with us all the way to Mo Bay. The story of a father unfaithful. An oft-told tale in Jamaica. But this particular father left Ernie's mother and moved next door and took up with the obeah woman who lived there. Her name was Mama Poon and she was, as they say, "dangerous". The word is drawn out, when spoken. Elongated. Scary sounding.

Ernie continued in English as if the story were too apocryphal for old Jamaican patois.

"Mi faddeh," he started, then switched, "My father, you see, he was a hero to the people of the village, and to us, too. He was the one who made the banana boats run because he could carry so many bunches at one time. He could hold two great heavy loads in his two big hands and still carry a hundred-hand-bunch on his head. He rowed out fast, too, like a motorboat, all the way out to the big ship called *The Producer* that loaded up and took the bananas to England.

"So he was a hero to all the village of Rockabess. To all of we!" he emphasized slipping back into his natural speech.

The story rolled on and on as we passed through the villages Ocho Rios (Ochy in local talk), down past the Bauxite docks in Discovery Bay, the sweet mangrove hideaway scattering of stilt houses in Falmouth, and so on all the way to Montego Bay.

But on the way I learned that Ernie's father lived side by side with his family, but never returned to his four children and his real wife, Ernie's mom. Never came back to the house he'd built, never gave them any money, though he made enough, never carried any responsibility for his own except for cutting their hair on a typical Sunday afternoon. That he did once each month, but nothing else. "Him cut the neighborhood children hair first," Ernie said. "We had to sit and wait our turn until end of day."

"How did you manage to survive?" I asked.

"I sell coconut figure."

He saw I didn't quite get it, and added, "I carved coconut birds, doves and doctorbirds and sold them to a man who worked at a hospital in Canada. I put food on the table with that handicraft."

I nodded. "So everyone in your family, the two girls and boys—they all worked at jobs and helped your mother."

"Yah, mon. That's how we live."

"What happened in the end?"

"The end?"

"Well, I mean, you're a grown man. Is your father still alive and living with Mama Poon?"

"Him dead. She dead."

That put a nail on the coffin, I thought, but he continued a little more as he parked the minibus at the airport.

"At the last we forgave him. He was in the hospital dying of cancer. His last days we brought him flowers and fruit and such, and his eyes filled with tears. All those long years he lived next door and never came over, but when his time came we went to Kingston and saw him in hospital and gave him real true love. For, after all, he was our father."

When we got out of the minibus and walked towards the airport, Ernie started to laugh. "There's a song we sing," he said. "A poem really, and it goes like this:

I know myself and I know my ways
And I will say with pride to the end of my days,
Praise God and my big right hand
I will live and die a banana man."

Chapter Twenty-Five

Laura was standing in the terminal when we came in.

There was a queue of gathered passengers babbling about an event on the plane. We couldn't quite catch what they were saying, something about an odd incident of some sort.

I introduced Ernie and we went to baggage claim, then to the Irie One. Then back up the coast road. Laura by my side, I knew everything was going to be all right.

"What happened on the plane?" I asked.

Laura always introduced things quietly. "There was a UFO," she said.

I thought she was kidding. She wasn't.

"It came right alongside us, all bright and twinkly-lighted...a large disk that came out of nowhere and vanished back into nowhere. It was the spookiest thing I have ever seen. People on the plane cried, gasped, shouted, sighed, fainted, and gagged. No one laughed. It was too real. Someone had to be revived—a woman fainted dead away and hit the carpeted aisle with a loud thud. She was fat. She was helped to her seat by attendants."

"Were you by the window?" I asked.

"I was close enough to see that the saucer had narrow-slitted windows. There were faces looking at us while we looked at them."

Ernie said, "How dem look so?"

Laura said, "Bone face. Best way I can describe it."

Then, she added, "It was exactly like the movies. They had elongated faces."

"What color?" I asked.

"Whitish, yellowish, greenish. Different colors."

Ernie burst out laughing. "So Jah seh. Technicolor people dem."

"How long did the saucer stay near the airplane?"

"No more than a few seconds. But it was so close I thought it would be a collision. It came out of a cloud."

"No wonder you looked funny when we picked you up in Mo Bay."

"What did I look like?"

"Like you'd just had a baby."

***

Ernie stopped at Northern Jerk, the chicken place. Full of bus drivers and the sound of cleavers banging on square wooden chopping blocks. The rising and falling and flashing of cleavers and the brown butcher paper wrapping and fast tying of string around small white square carboard boxes. And the smell of the fryers and the frying. The chicken place was intoxicating, even for one who eats so little meat. This was an indulgence for Laura and me, a luxury, a feeding frenzy.

And then we were back on the winding hemp-snake road where every time there was at least one horrible accident to witness. I'd seen my share of "deads" on this dangerous skinny road, full of sudden bony turns and the smell of threadbare tires and exhaust fumes.

There was a tuck shop bar called *One Stop* where we stopped for a ginger beer and I learned that this was popular no longer since Jamaican men heard that ginger lowered the sperm count or some such. Ernie said it was "fool-fool" but Jamaican men believed it and that settled it and the ginger beer industry was suffering on account of it.

After Falmouth there was much darkness on the road. But little cockroach cars with no tail-lights pulled out of hidden shell roads with deliberate blindness.

We continued to talk about the flying saucer all the way back. But when we got to the garage at Blue Harbour, there was a Russian Lada parked there with doors open.

A woman got out of the driver's side.

There was a loud bang that I thought was a firecracker. The woman fell face down and a man leaped out of the bushes.

He ran to the fallen woman and ripped the purse out of her hand.

Then he whirled around, almost colliding with the Irie One's front bumper.

At the same time, a small Morris station wagon came wheeling out of nowhere, gears grinding, cinders flying. The thief dived into the backseat, slammed the door, which bounced open again. Tires screaming, the Morris took off, its ruby red tail lights winking out of sight 'round the bend to Racecourse.

Chapter Twenty-Six

The wounded woman got to her feet. We couldn't find a blood spot on her.

She must have fainted, I thought. Then who got shot?

We found the woman's husband lying on his back by the cement wall that faced the sea one hundred feet below. He was shot in the arm. Dazed, but all right. The bullet had grazed his bicep. "Get me to a hospital," he said.

By now a half dozen people from Blue Harbour had shown up. There was Mark who laughed loud enough to wake the duppy dead. Dreamy, who was anything but. Ever present, almost invisible, Mackie. Pansy from Moneague in her dressiest dress, ready to go home by bus. Julie, great, big, strong Julie who could out-laugh the best of them. In any gathering of Jamaicans, there is always laughter, some jostling and fool-fool storytelling. This was no exception.

The police stood side by side in their blue pressed trousers and their pinstripe Jamaican cop-shirts with the short sleeves and epaulettes with gold buttons. Both men had cadet style hats, a mustache of the same neat length and thickness, broad backs, and stolid faces used to seeing things that weren't quite right.

This was obviously one of those things.

I thought of Laura, she'd barely gotten to her destination, and already, a shooting, a robbery and a UFO!

The police checked the shot man's arm and told the wife to drive him to the Port Maria hospital just down the road. One of them applied an ace bandage to stop bleeding while the other man scribbled in a palm-size notebook. Then they were gone and moments later, so were the wounded and unwounded tourists, both from Canada, as we presently discovered.

"That's wha dem get fi admire the view," Mark said, and laughed. His head went up and down when he laughed and his fake white teeth gleamed under the street lamp.

The party broke up. Laura and I stayed with Ernie. Mackie came out of the shadows of the old garage. The four of us said nothing. We stared at the curvature of the North Coast that ran twinkling all the way to Port Antonio which was thirty miles up coast, a corona of colored lights.

The sound of the ocean sea-washing the cliff wall was calming.

Laura talked a little about the UFO.

Mackie said, "We see dem all the while. Down at White River, over in Islington, near Friendship, up by Portland. People see dem, y'know. And dem tek people on dem ship dem." He moved his hands like a martial artist, gracefully describing the saucers circulating over the Jamaican hills.

"They good or bad?" I asked.

"Dem both. Same way. Just like we."

We left it that for the moment. Mackie and I carried Laura's bags up to the top of the veranda. Setting down the suitcase he was carrying atop his head, Mackie said, "When King Solomon son see him faddeh and tek the Ark of the Covenant it written that the Ark seem like it float just over the desert sand making a cloud of dust that them could see fi two thousand mile. Some seh that the first UFO inna Jamaica come down to earth and go into a hole in the reef out dere." He gestured towards Reef Pointe.

Ernie nodded. "Yah, mon. It real, it true. De hole inna de reef go straight to de bottom."

"The center of the earth," Mackie reminded. "Just like the mon, Nemo, tell us."

"Captain Nemo," Laura said from the open bedroom door. She'd changed into a light, loose blouse, now filled with wind from the sea so that she looked beautifully puffy.

"Him have a ship call *Nautilus*."

"He came to Jamaica?" Laura questioned. "Captain Nemo and his *Nautilus*?"

Ernie and Mackie nodded in unison and Ernie said, "Fi true, mon. Dem a come."

For a while we sat in the hard-backed Blue Harbour chairs. Carved of well-sanded, oiled mahogany and cedar from the sea, they were perfect for an all-night rapping session.

You could lean them back against the limestone block white washed walls and listen to the wind singing in your ear.

"Tomorrow," Mackie said, "Me tek you fi meet Sweet Sweet and him show you a mermaid ooman."

Maybe it was having Laura back in my arms in Sir Noel's four-poster that started it. Maybe it was Mackie's suggestion of Sweet Sweet and the mermaid woman.

Maybe it was just Jamaica, I don't know. But I dreamed of pink lights that streamed through my mind, that fairly howled and whistled and warbled and changed colors and tripped through me.

The streamers flowed like wine and went from pink to blue, and from blue to green, and from green to red. And with each sea change of color, I felt as though a whirling dervish, lighter than a feather, was dancing silk scarves across my naked skin.

Chapter Twenty-Seven

I woke in the very early morning and looked around the room. The wind was playing tag with the curtains. I shuddered. There was a little girl in a long Victorian nightdress playing around there.

Or was I dreaming?

She was sort of phosphorescent blue and she had long gold hair that went to the floor. When I looked directly at her, she vanished.

You had to look peripherally to see her.

After looking this way for a long time, I felt her draw closer to me. Finally, she was level with my head. She began running her fingers through my hair. I liked the way it felt and closed my eyes. Then I felt her tiny fingers on my eyelids, barely touching them, fingers soft as cotton.

I turned then, quite suddenly, and scared her.

She was gone.

I got up out of bed, and for a little while I did *qigong,* and watched Laura sleep.

The ghost girl had gone and I felt her absence.

Then it came to me, that with all the excitement, I'd forgotten my work.

I'd sent Len the last piece about quantum physics and the flashlight in the safe, but I was due to send him another one. I looked at my phone calendar: this, in fact, was the day the new essay was due.

I got my laptop and sat on Sir Noel's porch and typed the title: "The Saucer and the Shooter."

My point of view was that all phenomena came from the human eye and mind.

The moment I thought this, the little blue girl came back. Her long locks, her spirit fingers.

One direct look, and she was gone again.

Laura had said the same of the saucer visitation. It had only lasted a few seconds. The linear skeletal faces at the slit-windows of the saucer. There one second. Gone the next.

And what of the shooter? Too quick to see.

So, the quotient I was working with was Time. Whereas my other two pieces had delved into time-space-continuum. The inter-connection between those three concepts.

I was typing a stream of consciousness piece. What we used to call "automatic writing." Meaning, something that came from the unfiltered, unconscious mind.

I remembered my mystic friend, Fred. He had written to me when I first arrived in Jamaica. His words really touched me.

If a point
On a line
Has no
Magnitude
How can an infinite
Number
Of points
Be anything
But zero?
If a moment
In time
Has no
Width
How can
Moment
After moment

Add up to
A passage
Of time?

I wove Fred's time concept into what I was writing, and then re-titled it: *The Saucer, the Shooter,* and *the Passage of Time.* I tied it in at the end with Hemingway's short story (some consider it his best) *The Gambler, the Nun* and *the Radio.* It's not, I thought, that opposites attract. It's that opposites are not really opposites. They are part of the eternal weave of light and time.

No wonder Leonardo's Mona Lisa has smiled so long on canvas.

She is not a point in time.

Chapter Twenty-Eight

Laura and I ate breakfast upstairs on the veranda where I had just finished and faxed my essay to Len.

We were eating the most delicious cornmeal porridge in the world. Laura sweetened hers with sweet milk from a can, I dolloped molasses on mine. A flock of pocket parrots cheeped from a hollow almond tree.

Laura said, between spoons of porridge, "I could live here for as long as forever is."

If only I could keep her the way she looked that morning. Her sungold hair burning like a goddess. But, of course, as Fred said, there was no point of time to be held. Only the evanescent, poignant, passing moments.

We talked a little about Mackie as we drank a cup or two of Blue Mountain coffee.

"His last name is McDonnough, you know," she told me. "But his first name, while it sounds like it comes from the Mack in McDonnough, actually it's an African Twi word meaning, good morning. I mention this, because when I went downstairs to the kitchen, there he was smiling."

I asked, "He told you that?"

She nodded. "Mackie's ancestors are Ashanti."

"So he was born in the parish of St. Ann along with Bob Marley and Winston Rodney, better known as Burning Spear. But before them Marcus Garvey was born in St. Ann. That's a pretty impressive line-up."

She took another sip of Blue Mountain. "I spent some time with him after the shooting. The things he knows, he seems to know deeply. You know, as if everything were religion to him."

"That is the way with Rasta."

She set her cup on the wicker table next to us. A flock of red-headed parrots flew by arguing over something. Their sounds of ripping and rapping stopped us for a moment as they headed toward Mr Morris' place on the hill. They were going for the mangoes.

"Mackie's silences speak louder than his words," Laura said.

I mentioned, "He's taking us to meet a mermaid today."

Laura smiled, "He told me. It has something to do with another mystic man named Sweet Sweet."

"He's not so mystic," I said. "He's what they call *kas-kas*...and *teched*."

She gave me a curious stare.

"That means cuss-cuss, he swears a lot and is aggravated all the time. Teched means, according to Jah Son, touched." I tapped my forehead.

"You mean crazy?"

I nodded. "I heard Raggy call him a "coco head.""

"Which means?"

"Quirky, kwacky, wacky, and weird...and sometimes just plain foolish."

She said, "Tell me more. Where'd you get all these words?"

"I've been reading *Jamaica Talk* by Cassidy. It's the bible for patois. But anyway, a plain old stupid person they call a *bobo* and sometimes, if clownish, a *mumu*. Sweet Sweet can be either, or both, at the same time. He wasn't always like that though. Once he was smart and sensible. But after he met the mermaid, he became crazed."

"You've met him?"

"No, but I've heard him play the guitar. He plays it completely out of tune. He hammers it with his hand like it's a drum, all the notes discordant. His voice is quite pretty. He hits some bad notes, bass, falsetto, you name it. And that guitar just rasping and twanging and him playing chords that don't exist."

"What kind of music is it?"

"Old time 1940s calypso. What you might call fishing boat calypso, banana boat calypso. Kind of like American blues field songs. You know, those call and response songs. Sea hollers."

And then, as if we called him, and he responded, there was Mackie.

Chapter Twenty-Nine

"It go back," Mackie said. "Back to them old time when Columbus and them look fi gold."

We were driving through the little town of Castle Gordon, a town built around a Great House, a mansion from days of old. Ernie was at the wheel in the Irie One and Mackie was telling us about how Columbus and his men conscripted the Jews ejected from Spain.

This happened during the Inquisition. The wandering tribes were allowed to collect in a Columbus boat and they were transported to Jamaica. Under the trick of being called Portugals rather than Jews, these New World captives would dig for gold along with the Caribs and the Arawaks and Tainos.

"A whole heap of madness," Ernie said. "But so you get DaCosta... y'know 'im?"

He was referring to a family living in Castle Gordon. Two brothers, in particular. One nicknamed Pirate, the other called Tailor. "That an old, old line like Mackie mention," Ernie said. "Dem a-go back to pirate time."

"And so the nickname..." I said. They both laughed.

"True, true," Mackie said. "Pirate him mek mischief on the sea. Sometimes collect White Lady. Whole heap of White Lady."

I looked blankly at him.

"White Lady," Mackie said, "cocaine. Sometime dem dump a load inna plane. It fall inna de sea an' Pirate him capture it."

"First time it happen," Ernie said, laughing, "Him tink it powder paint and him mix wid seawater and paint him house white."

All three of us laughed at this. And by then we were at the house of Sweet Sweet who was playing his guitar on his porch. He wore a big woven sunhat.

He sang off key and so did his guitar.

But it was fascinating the "riddims" he coaxed out of that instrument which was a battered old six string from Schirmer's Music Store in Manhattan. Obviously a gift from someone.

Sweet Sweet had one good eye and one weak one. He spoke, so to speak, out of the good one, drilling you with it. You couldn't look away once he had you.

After singing a song about "man is an arrow, woman is a shadow" he got up, all lanky and loose, and went up a path behind his tucked in little house buried in bougainvillea.

It was just Laura and me and Mackie. Ernie stayed behind saying, "Me see 'er all the while," meaning that the mermaid was no friend of his.

The idea of a living, breathing mermaid was so fantastic, I expected to see a theatrical person in a costume.

Not so—what met our eyes was a pool of the lightest, milky green we had ever seen. Mackie sat on a stone and watched from a distance. That, all by itself, told us something.

Sweet Sweet was now down on all fours, singing a mermaid song. It was all about the golden table she sat on back in Columbus times. How the Spanish soldiers tried to trick her into coming closer so they could grab hold of the golden table. She rose up in the long ago, dripping silver tears. She was an innocent and they were cruel-hearted men searching for only one thing.

Sweet Sweet rapped the song out and the ripples in the pond multiplied.

Suddenly there was a swirl, a vortex of minnows.

It made us dizzy to follow them with our eyes.

"Don't do that," Sweet Sweet hollered. "That how she vex you."

Suddenly her head appeared. Her hair was as long as the fins that kept her aloft. She was blonde as the sun. Her hair rose and fell as the minnows propelled themselves in spirals all around her.

"Wha are you doin' here?" she said, her full lips dripping. Her long taffy-colored hair spread out and virtually covered the circumference of the pond.

I was staring in disbelief. So was Laura.

Sweet Sweet was sitting in the grass, smiling.

The mermaid had brown skin with a queer greenish cast to it. It fluctuated from the color of grass to the color of copper. Her face was a beautiful oval with her lovely eyes well-set apart. Her open mouth was full of tiny, barracuda teeth.

"Dem me children," she announced, nodding towards the crescents and curves made by the school of minnows. "Wha ya go do? Eat dem?"

Her brown eyes caught me staring at the children.

"You belly empty an' dat why you a-come fi me place."

I said nothing. Laura and I were in a complete state of disbelief.

I felt I had been slipped a drug, or maybe this was a clever trickster's illusion. Maybe Sweet Sweet was a necromancer. An obeah man.

My head was pounding from the sun. I blinked.

"You tink me scare?" she asked.

Her voice was soft as water.

I shook my head.

She said in a sharp voice, "Tell me, bwai, what you eat?"

I was hypnotized by the gyre of spinning minnows.

I stuttered. "I, I, I…"

"Ya no touch fresh, only salt," Sweet Sweet said, chuckling.

She didn't seem to hear him, but her suspicious eye remained on me.

Laura whispered in my ear. "Tell her you eat only salt."

"Saaaalt!" I said in a sudden protracted stammer.

"Salt, ya seh. Den ya no eat me beeby dem."

I smiled faintly. My head was still ringing from the sun, the swirling minnows, the milk water pond turning like a prayer wheel.

"Ya tink me scare of you, bwai?"

"No, no, nooo."

Now she smiled, very faintly. Her little white fangs gleaming. So incongruous in her tan lovely flesh. Her breasts, full and bare, nipples round and brown. The fiery halo of her locks spread like a sequined shawl. The tawny lion-colored skin of her upper body and her breasts softly bobbing in the water and the amber undulations of darting minnows and the sunshine fire wheel the spokes dizzying in their rotations.

I felt myself coming apart, quailing before an apparition of beauty and nightmare.

I looked at Laura.

The sun was gone.

It was night.

Was I still alive?

The thing called heart was strong in me.

I heard a repetitive gong.

A river roared.

I babbled, "Salt, salt, salt."

Chapter Thirty

In the dream-swoon I heard Mackie's voice, telling Ernie and Laura about heart.

Long ago, he said, Mother Earth met with her brothers and sisters. There was Sun, Moon, Dark, Rain and Heart.

Mother Earth said, I am going away for a little while. So I must ask you what you will do to care for things while I'm gone.

Rain spoke in a rush. I will rain down on the earth with all my strength.

Mother Earth said, So everything on earth will be under water.

Rain nodded and withdrew with a wet hiss.

Sun came up next and said, I will send out the hottest of my rays to everyone and everything.

Mother Earth said, In that way, everything alive will wither and die.

Sun sank and disappeared.

Then Dark said, I will wrap the world in shadow.

Mother Earth said, your shadow, being everywhere, will blind all things so no one will see anything.

Dark faded away and disappeared.

Moon was next to say, My gentle light will rule softly and no one will mind.

Mother Earth said, Such gentleness will tire us out because there will be no rest from it.

Moon grew thin and all but vanished.

One person was left, Heart.

Heart said, I have no idea how to be, I only know how to feel.

Mother Earth asked, How is that?

Heart said, No one should be left out or left in, as brothers and sisters we should all work together not apart.

Mother Earth asked, What will you feel when I am not here?

Heart said, I will miss you.

Mother Earth said, Heart you shall always be present to remind your brothers and sisters that they must work together in harmony.

Then Mother Earth went on her journey and she was gone for one sunny day, one rainy day, one moony night, and one dark night.

When she returned everything was just as it had always been and would always be because Heart was there and all the brothers and sisters were heartful.

Chapter Thirty-One

That dream folded into a second dream. In that one Ernie was telling Mackie and Laura his version of the Heart Story. It went like…

"If old Lady Bug lights on your arm," he said, "that's good luck. So you must spit on her and if she don't come back, it's more good luck."

"What if she do come back?" Mackie asked.

"Well, if she do come back, that's very bad luck," Ernie said, "but you have to remember when you spit pon her, you have to say this likkle poem:

> *Lady Bug, Lady Bug*
> *Fly away, don't come back*
> *Another day"*

"Well, that's what they say anyway," Ernie said, laughing.

Then he sighed and said, "I don't know nothing about no ladybug business, bad luck good luck, you got to choose your own luck."

Mackie laughed, and said, "When the rain a-fall it don't fall on one man's house alone. Bob Marley said that, same time, he told me everything have a purpose, find a reason, for every season…"

I woke up then and Mackie was there and he handed me an old leather-bound Bible.

"I marked the verses for you," he said.

"Why?"

"Mermaid protection."

Chapter Thirty-Two

"There is another spring," Mackie said, "down in Priory where I come from."

We were sitting in the sun down by the old pool, the one dug by Sir Noel when he first moved to Blue Harbour to escape the British tax laws.

The pool was built right in the sea. Hand-dug. Then a sea wall was made for protection, so that the pool was saltwater, drawn in through holes in the sea wall. In a rough sea you could still swim there, but you risked sea anemones and sometimes stinging men of war.

Mackie gave me a June plum. "Present for Laura," he said.

I put the plum in the upper pocket of my fishing shirt.

"What about the other spring you mentioned?"

Mackie smiled. "No one ever notice it much except on a moon night. But I notice it all the while. The thing is, the pool have some natural chemical, gas maybe, that do something fi de skin."

He motioned toward my hands. I saw them for the first time in days. So many things had happened I'd forgotten to look. The fur was thicker than ever. The hands looked like Stevenson's Mr Hyde, hairy and misbegotten.

"All right," I said, "let's go to Priory. How far?"

"Nuh far, mon."

Mackie had often spoken about Priory as a special place. For one thing, the Columbus ship, as he put it, was sunk there. The timbers still visible in 20 feet of water. For another, Burning Spear was there. I liked the name Priory, the antique sound of it.

We went there. Hiked from the town to a jungled shelf of limestone rock. Wherein lay a little pool, hidden by dwarf palms. It also was protected by a copse of ghost bamboo. A secret pool to be sure.

"Some people bathe with just their face in it," Mackie said. He scratched a wooden match on the limestone outcropping, and tossed it into the water.

Quickly the surface of the tranquil water became agitated, and quixotically, danced with blue flames.

I stared in disbelief.

"Is it gas, Mackie?"

"No mon."

"Has to be," I said. "Water doesn't burn."

"Dis water bun," Mackie in patois to emphasize his point.

"What happens if you get in it?"

"Nuttin."

"Serious?"

"It not even hot, mon. Just warm."

I looked at my malevolent hands. Had the tropics inspired and quickened that mad growth of thick black hair? I was more beast than man.

"Put your hands in, Jack," he said.

I pulled off my fishing shirt, put my left hand into the twisting blue twining flames. The water was warm, not hot, but I still retracted my hand as if it might grow hotter and burn me.

Looking at my hand, I couldn't believe it…almost all of the crazy hair was gone. I'd felt no heat from the flames, but whatever was in the curative water had eaten away the pernicious hair.

I tried it again with my right hand. Then both.

"Leave your hands in," Mackie suggested.

I did.

"Now pull them out."

I did.

Hairless.

Completely shiny me.

"Do it again," Mackie advised.

They came out unscathed but devoid of hair.

I burst out laughing. "No more golfing gloves," I said.

"No mon," Mackie said with a quick grin.

He bent down and lit a Craven-A cigarette off the flickering blue lights.

He handed it to me and I drew on it deeply.

When I released the smoke I understood why he'd given the cigarette to me. It was a ceremony and I was letting something evil go out of me. Banishing something malign inside myself. Something that had been haunting me for weeks. Now it went away on the soft wings of smoke.

I was restored.

"Thank you, Mackie. My hands are back the way they were, and it didn't even hurt."

He gave me a small green coconut as a celebratory gift.

I passed it from one palm to the other, feeling its smoothness and weight. Then I gently and effortlessly squeezed the coconut and it cracked like an egg.

Chapter Thirty-Three

So, as it turned out, my hands were even more powerful than before.
They were fur-free, clean, and supernaturally strong.

The myth of Samson in reverse.

It was an eerie feeling, having hands that could crack a coconut.

Back at Blue Harbour, I waited to see if Laura would notice I wasn't wearing my golfer's gloves. But she didn't seem to see the gloves were gone.

When I held my hands in front of her face, she stared in surprise. Then she took hold of one and rubbed it against her cheek. "No more bristle," she said. "How did you do it?"

"Burned it off at the Librium Hot Spring in Priory."

"They're beautiful hands again, the way they always were. The creature is gone."

She shook her head in disbelief.

"But are they just as strong?" she wondered.

"Do you see that old, rusted iron they use for a doorstop?"

"Yes."

I walked over to it, picked it up and tore the iron end off. It felt like a piece of cardboard.

She gave me a worried look. "You won't hurt anyone, will you?"

"Not unless they hurt me, or you, first."

That night, walking in the Maypan moonlight of the coconut farm at the bottom of the property, I had one of those weird moments where everything you're made of is tested.

I was walking in the cool night air noticing the way the Maypans shadowed the path. Their frilly pointed fingers of shadow moved in the sea wind and then a man stepped into the center of the path. He had a cudgel made of lignum vitae, the toughest wood there is.

The shadow man stood there rapping the cudgel on his open palm.

I said, in a voice not quite my own, "You don't want to do this."

To me, my voice sounded deeper than usual.

I glanced at interloper's face. It was obscured by a bandana that covered everything but his eyes.

"You're being a bit dramatic, don't you think?"

But as soon as I said this he came rushing at me.

He was quick as a cat and he made two swipes with the cudgel before I could step back out of his way. I took one blow on the forearm before my right hand, of its own volition, seized his cudgel.

For a moment the shadow man and I grappled with the weapon. Then my left hand swung in an arc and caught the other end of the cudgel. With no effort I wrestled it from the attacker's hands and struck him a blow on the head that felled him in the guinea grass. Then my hands, of their own volition it seemed, snapped the cudgel in half, and pitched it away into the moonlight night.

Two more men, similarly attired in darkness, came from either side of the Maypan path. This time I was the aggressor. Running at the one on the left, I dodged his night stick, felt it graze my shoulder as I ducked. Pain shot down my side. At the same time, however, my hands sunk into the man's left leg and upended him, as if he were a piece of balsa wood. Then I tossed him. He landed hard, crying out as he connected with the rocky ground.

There was yet another fool who came at me like a bull. I took a dozen blows, head and shoulder, before I could get in close. Then the hands did their work. I heard his elbows crack. They dangled deadweight. Both hands took his head just above the ears and…I remembered the coconut. "No more," he whimpered. The hands let go. He dropped.

111

Then it was as if nothing had happened.

There were little chirps from hidden birds. A pocket parrot chittered at being awakened. There were groans in the darkness, furtive dragging sounds. I saw one of them hobbling down by the old pool. The first man was still out cold. The third was moaning in a tangle of bramble. I could hear him trying to crawl like a lizard.

I sat down on a fallen Maypan log. As I meditated, the three faded from my consciousness. It was as if the Samson hands had willed it to be so. Showing me what was, what wasn't. What was to be, and not to be. And it all went away just as it should, as if it hadn't happened.

I got up and walked. A little further on the moon path, I stood under the great almond trees with their huge copper-colored, ready to drop leaves.

I felt my heart. It was not beating fast or hard. Whatever had just happened had occurred without even a hint of effort or sweat.

Then a fourth figure of darkness appeared from behind the greatest almond tree of all. The Father of the Forest, I had heard people say. A tree as old as the limestone hills themselves.

"Beg you a mawney?" the man, standing white in the moon, asked.

"I didn't quite hear that," I said.

"Me need a mawney," he said.

"A mawney…you bruk?"

"Me bruk," he said, and began to weep.

I listened to him for a while, wondering what to say or do.

I had no wallet, no money.

But there he was standing there in the moon's pale paint, with his hands out begging for succor.

It was my hands again that couldn't resist. The nimble fingers undid the buttons of my old Jamaican Army shirt, the one given me by Morris Tailor, the DaCosta brother.

The hands of the beggar reached out and took the shirt and hastily put it on.

I realized then that the man was stark naked.

Yet now he had a shirt and the shirt nearly covered most of his nakedness, as he was a small man.

"Me need a trouser," the man said.

Again, the hands undid my pants, I stepped out of my old New Mexico jeans.

The beggar grabbed the pants.

Soon he was clothed. I was the one who was bare, but for a pair of silk Rasta shorts—red, green and gold—that I had bought at the open air market two days earlier.

"You all right?" I asked, feeling the sea breeze tickle my body.

He shook his head. "Me need a likkle work," the man said.

"Ask Mackie inna the morning," I told him.

He nodded, then said, "You are a Christian mon."

I said, "No, I am a Rastamon."

It was the first time I had ever said that…to anyone, including myself.

"You bless," the man said. "Naked came I and you clothed me."

I said goodbye under the immense tear-shaped leaves and the enormous snake-like roots of the towering almond tree.

I never saw him again.

But when I got back to our apartment on the upper veranda, I saw that Mackie's Bible had been fluttered by the invisible fingers of the sea wind.

I looked and it was open to a passage in Proverbs 28, Verse 17: "Iron sharpeneth iron; so a man sharpeneth the countenance of his friend."

The wind pulsed, flipped pages.

Then the wind softened and the Bible was open to Jeremiah, Chapter One, Verse 19:

"And they shall fight against thee; but they shall not prevail against thee; for I am thee, saith the Lord, to deliver thee."

Chapter Thirty-Four

I slept briefly on the veranda. But I kept hearing in my head, "iron sharpeneth iron."

I would wake and see Mackie, his teak face like an African mask. The furrows on either side of his face running river-like. His eyes, almond shaped, penetrating deep into me.

He wasn't there, in that bamboo chair where he liked to sit, but I saw him in my dream, waiting for me to wake. That, in itself, would wake me.

I never met a man like him. A man more in touch with the rhythm of nature; the rhythm of himself in nature. There was no doubt in him. No hidden tension. He swam in and out of shadows. He knew whereof he swam and wherefore he would go. There was no wonder or expectation in him. What he didn't know, wasn't worth knowing. He was entirely in the present moment.

When he spoke deep he made the floorboards buzz. His patois flew like sparks. But his phrases depended on his moods. He reserved pinging patois for emphasis. Otherwise, his voice was low and rich and convincing without being threatening.

He wasn't there as I sat on Sir Noel's rocking couch dozing and waking. But I felt his presence anyway.

He was everywhere.

He was nowhere.

No one ever knew where he was, and then, there he would be before you. I believed he could be invisible when he wanted to be.

There was a ringtone then and I answered it. My editor Len Coppard asked. "Where's your story for *Aquamaze*?"

I explained I was on various locations, gathering material. We concluded with me promising a new story by 9AM.

Then, after the call, I was writing it to the rhythm of the sea. I was wide awake, writing a piece called, "The Mermaid Meridian."

It came easily for it was straight autobiographical truth, but I also added two myths Mackie told me.

One was a man who had been captured by a mermaid and then married by King Neptune. It sounded childlike until it turned sexual.

The lost sailor breathed air that lasted in his lungs for days—part of the mermaid's magic. Her mesmeric spell included many uncanny sexual adventures with the two of them making love among the corals and sea creatures. It was mythical, poetical and sometimes absurd.

Being a sailor with lots of human foibles, the lost sailor sought other maids of the fin variety—goldheads, redheads, and other beauties, and in the end, he was kicked, or flipped, out of underwater Eden, and thus he spent the rest of his life sorrowing over his lost love beneath the sea. An oft told tale, but freshly sprinkled with Caribbean aphorisms.

Naturally, Mackie told it better than I can, and with less abstraction. For him the story was plain and simple, and true as told. It had happened.

"Mermaids have powers," he said. "Far beyond the waters where they live."

Then he explained that the Mermaid bible came from the goddess Erzulie. She was a descendent of the ancient ones. Her laughter and the laughter of the mer-people that served her could easily, he insisted, bewitch a human. One had to be careful of mermaid dreams. Red was the worst color in a mermaid dream. Green and blue the best. But pink, he said, was dangerous because it could turn to red. Such colors could raise you up into the holy firmament or crush you under the weight of an evil spell.

I put all of this in my story, which was a little longer than usual, then I went downstairs to the living room and faxed it.

An hour later, Len phoned me.

116

"M likes it," he said. "Keep going with the psychic, the mysterious, the unbelievable. Send more. Don't lose yourself over there. You're working for us, remember. Maybe two stories a week now?"

I said, "Two is a lot."

He responded, "Get off the weed."

"I'm not on it."

He wrote, "Then this stuff you're writing is true?"

"It is, Len."

"I worry about you then."

"I do too."

I wondered if, like Sweet Sweet, I was now "teched."

***

If I had to, I could handle two stories a week, with each about 2500 words. But I didn't want to be bossed around. On the other hand, they hadn't bossed me. They'd permitted me to live in paradise. I just had to keep my head screwed on tight.

On the other hand, if I did that, would I become inaccessible to the magic and the mysterious events that seemed to be happening every day.

I was writing better than I ever had in my life. It was "spirit of place." The other ingredient was…something else. I didn't know what.

The mermaid magic?

Sometimes I thought I was dreaming when I was awake. Sometimes, awake, I thought I was dreaming.

You know you're going crazy when you see a knot in a pandana basket and it looks like an old pirate winking at you. Worse, a piece of used toilet paper carries the brown outline of a soldier from the war of 1812.

Some of this became clearer when Mackie and some other Blue Harbour friends took us on a trip to the little town of Friendship where a woman named Mrs Pett did séance and crystal readings. She read minds, Mackie said, like a newspaper. He would not go inside the house, but waited outside, as did Ernie.

Mrs Pett lived in a tiny little wooden house on a hill. White clapboard with Victorian curlicue trim.

I had told Len where I was going, and why, and he did a strange thing. He, or most likely, M, arranged for the séance to be filmed. A crew from a documentary film company showed up at the same time we did.

The producers, Tim and Ally, were friendly and nice. Very easy going. The camera men were edgy and annoyed because there was no electric outlet and the only light was kerosene lanterns. To film the séance, they drew power from a small self-contained generator, but it didn't allow for more than an hour of interview time.

Mrs Pett and her husband resembled Ike and Tina Turner of Motown fame. He wore a white silk suit and had a pencil thin mustache and looked a trifle evil. She was gracious and beautiful. She also had more than a little charisma in her white turban, Caribbean head-wrap. Her dress emphasized her full breasts, small waist, and acres of flowing white silk going in different directions.

The film folks rubbed their hands together and grinned. "It can't get better than this," Ally said.

And began recording the moment by moment revelations of Mrs Pett, while her husband sat immobile on a chintz, Sir Noel era sofa. His lips never moved, nor did any other body part that we could see.

"So," she started off, "You first." She pointed a well-manicured, ruby red finger nail at me and tapped me once on the breastbone. Then she held a candle flame before my face and told me to look deeply into it while she recited the names of arcane saints.

"In the name of Saint Marron, Saint Legba, Mistress Erzulie, Saint Samson, Saint Affagaffagaff, Saint Umbilical, Saint Bullwinkle, Saint

Smokey." The saintly list went on and on. I couldn't remember half the names. When she stopped her recitation, she took me by the hand, led me to the back porch of the house. She showed me what she called "The feast of the Saints."

I glanced at an infernal pile of guts and horns, a fly-ridden mess of red, rotten, purple and black meat.

"That is what I feed the saints," she whispered, "and they in turn feed me with information of a spiritual kind."

I nodded and then she took me back inside, where my stomach reeling, I readjusted myself to the situation. I was glad the cameramen had not tried to follow us out there.

"You may not leave the island," she said to me, "unless I give you leave."

I said nothing. But in my head, I could hear Len Coppard saying, "She's priceless, stay on top of this."

The candle and the hungry saints visited each face in the room.

She asked Hucky, the wayward, woebegone storyteller of the group, "How come you sleep with the dead?"

He shrugged, "Me no know."

She said, "You know. Admit it. They rule you. Is not your wife who runs things. Is a whole heap of ghost!"

Hucky shivered visibly all over. He hid his face in his hands.

Ernie stuck his head in the door to see what was going on, and she said in a commanding tone, "You come in here now."

She did the saint rap, the candle inquisition. Then Mrs Pett told Ernie, "You nuh here, mon. Yuh here, in body only. Yuh spirit gone a-foreign. Unnerstand?"

Ernie looked around the room in anguish.

At the same time, a tiny bat flew in and out through the open veranda door.

The documentary film people laughed, all of them.

"Mek him spirit come and go," Mrs Pett said. "Mek him go direct fi stateside where him belong."

I saw Ernie begin to shake. Then he tripped over a camera stanchion on the floor, and beat it out of there, with everyone in the room laughing out loud. The Ike Turner husband laughed with everyone else and I saw his buff white teeth and his snaky mustache.

She turned back to me. "Yuh must stay until me tell you fi go. Awright?"

I said, "No problem."

Lastly she told the fortunes of the producers, Tim and Ally.

To him, she said, "You land hard on the floor when you get home."

This was followed by more laughter from everyone.

To her, she said, "You turn believer by sunrise."

When we left, shortly thereafter, the filmmakers paid her $100 U.S. and I did the same.

And for the first time, I noticed that her pretty face was wet with sweat and her make-up beginning to smear.

Outside, when we headed toward Ernie's minibus, I noticed a large brown cow chewing cud in the front yard. As they were leaving, every-one patted the cow, but me. I leaned down and said into its stiff, starched ear, "What are you doing here?"

The cow chewed cud, green slime leaking from its mouth.

"Look out for the Annexerians," it said.

I said, "Iron sharpeneth iron."

Chapter Thirty-Five

Mrs Pett was right on all counts.

She may have been theatrical, but she was accurate in her vision of each person in the room; their ways, their addictions and afflictions.

Hucky admitted in the minibus that he had been imagining there were ancient voices in his bedroom. He said, "At night I see duppy from the past, them old relation who nuh leggo. Sometime them even nyam in bed when me try to sleep. Inna the morning, crumbs everywhere on the bed sheet."

"Them nyam hard dough bread all night and them give me nuttin."

The film people stayed the night at Blue Harbour and Ally, the associate producer got kicked out of bed and landed on the floor. She wasn't sleeping with anyone. "I leave you all to the duppies and psychics and psychos, the shooters and mermaids, and whatevers. This is a crazy place and I'm going home to nice little old provincial Los Angeles where nothing ever happens."

She added, "Sad to say, the rushes last night of the Mrs Pett Show came out too dark to see. There were unaccountable white spots in the film, too."

Hucky told me later that those white spots were duppies traversing the room. He also told me that he'd been followed home by a UFO, a small one, a two-seater, glowing like a giant peenywally or firefly.

In Jamaica everyone has a story.

The following day things quieted down and Laura and I went shopping at the local market. I heard a big, happy, fat woman singing, "Hey, Mister, touch me tomato, touch me pumpkin, potato."

The higglers and sellers were everywhere, their garden goods and foods spread out on burlap sacks for all to see. Huge rough yams, some the size of footballs, strings of tangerines, carpets of round green limes, naseberries, soursops, sweetsops, oranges, ackee and callaloo.

Julie and Pansy picked and pointed, and I carried out to Mackie and the minibus.

Bend down low, so I can tell you what I know.

I bent down low to pick up a sack of heavy potato and my canvas pants split up the middle and I had no belt so my pants went down to my ankles and everyone in the open air market roared with laughter. A brass button white man with his pants down...

But best of all, for everyone to see, was that I was wearing my red, gold and green silk BVDs. It was like I had the Ethiopian royal flag around my waist and the Emperor, Haile Selassie I, Himself, was saluting me from the top of a lofty palm tree. I pulled my pants up and a chuckling higgler handed me a string of hemp to hold up the belt loops and tie myself in place.

While tying, the sea breeze cooled my lower parts. I was air conditioned from belly button to bum. All in a day's work. Duppy spots by night, higgler giggles by day. What was I coming to? Where had I gone to?

Mackie sidled up to me and said in his grave, deep voice, "Dem wid you now, mon. Dem is one wid you."

True, the eyes smiled, grinned, guffawed wherever I went that day.

That night Tony Delmohamid, an East Indian Jamaican, dropped by and told us a story no one could ever forget.

He had Chuckie, a local character, with him. The two together were like the Fox and the Cat in *Pinocchio*, both telling tales and snickering in between, and then Tony grew solemn and said, "The drum gets thirsty, too, y'know."

He poured a little white rum, which flashed in the moonlight, on top of his goatskin repeater drum. He then rubbed it on the head of the drum, his fingers moving in a steady circular fashion.

After doing this for a while, he struck the drumhead a couple of times, and said, "Yah, mon, that is a happy sound."

He made some furtive movements with his spidery hands.

"I am pouring a dram for the earth," he said. "She get thirsty too."

Then, "And one for my cousin, the lucky one we called the Duke of Ocho Rios."

His face became taut and sad. I saw a tear in his eye.

He poured the dram for the Duke and corked the bottle with a hard palm down pat. "They say the mind doesn't see what the heart don't leap."

Tony's large eyes were trained on me. "I hear you lose your trousers today," he said, and then he and Tony and Hucky and Mackie started to laugh.

I joined them, so did Laura.

For a moment, we were the laughing fool-fools of Castle Garden.

And then, as abruptly the laughter started, it stopped.

"Another dram for Duke," Tony said.

Tony spoke the King's English, if he wished.

And he wished now.

"You would have to know Duke to understand why he was the luckiest man on earth. He knew what it meant to be alive. He was poor and humble and simple in his needs and he lived to help others. No one begrudged him anything. He had a lovely wife and daughter and his life was like something out of a book, but one day, walking down a back street in Ocho Rios, someone fired a shot at someone else and the bullet struck Duke and ended his life. Right there on the street, dead for good dead. No more Duke."

The only sound in the moonlit yard was that of the cheeping tree-frogs.

Tony continued. "Whatever Duke had he shared. He was always sharing what he had and what he knew. Every moment was special when you were with him. He just seemed to glory in life. He took nothing for granted. People's luck changed when they were near him, which is why they called him "The Duke Of Luck" because he brought that good luck to others. All who knew him were blessed. When I touch the earth tonight and give him this little blessing from all of us, I am touching Duke's lucky heart, for that is where we all reside tonight, in his heart of hearts."

I heard voices saying, "Yes I".

Others said, "Righteousness."

Some said, "Guidance."

One sang out, "To the Most High."

I waited for the quiet to return and after a while it did and I asked Tony, "Where is the spirit of Duke right now?"

Tony's eyes filled with tears. "Tonight," he said, "I was down on Pagee Beach and I felt his spirit pass through. I knelt down and asked Duke for help. Help me see the light, I said.

And then I hear his voice. He say softly, "Go into the sea."

I did this thing.

The moon was on the water and the sea was clear.

"Reach down and take the blessing for each and for all."

I hear him say that, and then I look into the water and see pearls. Hundreds of pearls there at my feet in the sand.

I believe I am having a vision. These silvery pearly are not real.

But Duke say again: "Truly, now, take my blessing, pass around to all who knew me."

Hours it take to gather the pearls, Tony said.

At Blue Harbour the voices rose in unison.

"Irie."

"Jah bless."

"Love."

"May the eyes of the most high be upon us."

"May Lucky Duke be with us."

"Always, all ways, and all of our days."

Each man made his own offering of smoke, herb, leaf of life, white rum, something sacred. Something of value.

Then the velvet silence.

The chiming tree frogs.

The scraping croakers.

The sea carving rocks.

Finally, the voices of the prayerful woven into one harmonic voice:

> *By the rivers of Babylon*
> *Where we sat down*
> *And there we wept*
> *When we remembered Zion*
> *For the wicked carried us away*
> *To captivity*
> *And required of us a song*
> *But how can we be singing*
> *In a strange land.*

The drums, no longer thirsty, rang out over the mountain.

And we heard other drums, far off, answer.

Before I left the drum circle, I asked Tony

"The pearls were real?"

"Yah, mon," he said.

I looked into his eyes.

He made a fist and gently touched his heart four times.

"And you knew it was Duke…but how did you know it was him?"

Tony smiled. "Others have asked me that. The hands that gathered the pearls were my own hands. But when I looked at them in the watery moonlight, I saw that they were his hands not mine."

"But how did you know?"

"His hands were scarred by a bicycle chain when we were very young."

"So they were his hands that got the pearls."

Tony nodded. "Everyone in the village has some now. I gave them all away except for the ones I gave to Duke's wife and daughter. They got more. I did what he would have done."

"Have you seen or felt his spirit since?"

Tony tapped his heart four times.

"There is no separation from him, or me, or you and I. We are all one. But that being the simplest truth is the hardest truth to accept."

Mackie knelt down and spoke, "As it seh in Psalm 77, I cried unto God with my voice…and he gave ear unto me…"

Mackie's voice dropped even lower. We saw a flicker of lightning far out in the bay by Hurricane Allen Reef Point. He said, "Thy way is in the sea, and thy path in the great waters, and thy footsteps are not known."

"So these that you hear are the dark sayings of old," Mackie said. "Duke was no more than a man. But so was Jesus who also came from the sea and walked upon it."

He opened his hand and there was a pearl in it.

Chapter Thirty-Six

From fourteenth century to twenty-first century, literature has offered us many pearls of one kind or another to show humankind that the only real pearl of value is the human heart.

The pearl was innocence, purity, beauty, perfection.

And always there was the Devil to squander it. To tempt with it. To use it for corruption of goodness.

The fourteenth century Middle English story written in stanzas is about the dream of a father who mourns the loss of his pearl. In the dream he sees the Pearl Maiden standing across a stream standing across a strange landscape. He questions her, and she shows him a vision of the Holy City of Jesus Christ.

A document of morality and of the permanence of the afterlife, the medieval pearl tale is visionary and prophetic.

No less so, I thought, waking from my own pearl dream fashioned from threads of the night before.

I told Laura about it and she said, "You go to all these places and I'm not even awake yet."

"That's what dreams do," I said.

We breakfasted that morning on the well-known bun-and-cheese of Jamaica. This is a spiced bun with a yellow cheese. This, plus Blue Mountain coffee, was a perfect way to start the day. We polished off slices of cold Julie Mango served, in this case, by none other than a Julie.

I have said nothing about Julie and Pansy, who basically ran the main house of Blue Harbour. Pansy was a retired teacher. Not because she wanted to be but because she needed to support her family and there was a living wage as a housekeeper but, in Jamaica, no supporting wage for a teacher at that time.

Pansy, like her name, was a flower of the Moneague hills. She could describe a car wreck, delicately and artistically. The rise and fall of her voice always reminded me that poetry rides the horse called patois.

Once Pansy said to me, "The horses of youth run fast, but the asses of experience amble thoughtfully."

She was like that. Though young, she moved thoughtfully like an older, wiser person. The way she treated others was thoughtful as well. I believe that her aunt who lived with her family was an influence, as it must be in all Jamaican families. Laura said, that same morning, "The people you like the most in Jamaica have elders living with them."

I told her something my father used to quote from Shakespeare, "Even with a fool something rubs off." He also said, "Youth is wasted on young people." Both things rang true in the small villages of the North Coast. Iron sharpeneth iron.

Julie was big and strong and smiled the day long. Yet when she was sad everyone in the surrounding hills knew about it. I found her crying a few times, alone in the kitchen, over some lost thing. Some pearl that had slipped away into the cracks of despondency. Then she was as sorrowful as she was large.

Once she was standing barefoot in back of the kitchen on a path strewn with Flame of the Forest flowers fallen from a sudden shower. She was wiping her eyes with her apron. "What's wrong?" I asked.

"I need mawney bad," she said. "Not for me, for my daughter, Tanicia."

I saw something shining beneath her big toe.

I pointed to it. "What is that?"

She stooped and picked it up, the tears still wet on her face.

Then she nodded and smiled. "A message," she said.

It was only a bright, shiny quarter.

But, to Julie, in that tearful moment, it was a pearl of infinite value.

Chapter Thirty-Seven

Things began to happen at Blue Harbour that hadn't happened before.

A strange character called by the locals, "The Israel", moved into the lower level Sir Noel cottage named Villa Rose.

There he held court. We could hear him from our upper veranda. His voice was loud and resonant and he spoke the finest patois ever spoken by a white foreigner. The Israel always had an audience from Castle Gordon.

He came from Israel, and as we learned, he was a deserter from the Israeli army. The Israel had a habit of telling everyone what to do. Mostly people obeyed him. Mackie told me he'd once been in his bedroom at Villa Rose and the man's attaché case was wide open revealing tens of thousands of dollars. Currencies from all over Europe. "Him a tief," Mackie said with finality. "Don't turn your back on him."

One night while The Israel was holding a loud-mouth court below our bedroom and we couldn't sleep, Laura and I went walking up the hill to get away from the verbal bushwhacking that was going on.

"I don't understand why they even listen to him," I told Laura.

She said, "Then you don't understand how Adolf Hitler appealed to millions of Germans."

I chuckled at this. She was right, as usual. The Israel was a Jewish Adolf assembling his make-believe army.

"You think his little army will grow?" I asked Laura.

"It has grown already," she said. "Sometimes twenty or thirty men are down there on his terrace. He blabs in town too. People are mesmerized by him."

We walked uphill until we came to Mackie's little pepper garden.

I had never noticed it before but now I saw in the starlight a narrow goat path leading well above the sea and curving towards Ochy.

We followed it.

Soon we found ourselves on a different property. A mysterious old stone house, somewhat devasted by storms, was set against the headland hill.

The house was dark and forbidding.

We had left one evil and found another.

I put my hand on the medicine bag I now carried around my neck. The pahos in it, the sacred feathers, were my tangible pearl guardians.

We moved forward in a sea wind that seemed to be pushing us toward the broken down, old mansion.

Suddenly there was a cry near the guango tree

Chapter Thirty-Eight

A man was bent over a small firepit, stirring a brew of some kind, chanting.

"I wondered when you would come," he said in clear English.

We came close to the fire. "Si-dung," he said in patois.

We had gotten good at the aboriginal squat which seemed to fit every nightly visitation. Our meetings with remarkable men, finned women, and obeah women, masterminds of darkness, all of them. They seemed to be multiplying.

This man, I seemed to realize, was the quintessential one.

"Si-dung," he repeated. "And have a drink of immortality."

Whatever this meant, we obeyed, though Laura said, "We can only stay a minute or two."

At this the man laughed.

He was, I could see in the firelight, of average size. His face was chiseled and his eyes were like knives, narrow and crafty. His fingers were long and thin.

"Don't tell me about yourself," he whispered. "I already know."

"How is that?" Laura asked reasonably. "We haven't ever been here before."

"The messenger told me about you."

"What messenger?" I asked.

"The old man in the desert. That one you call Sungazer."

I felt rivulets of chills run up and down my arms.

We squatted and listened to the snap-crack of the fire.

The peenywallies and blinkies carved the space all around us.

The man saw me looking, turning my head to see them.

"We call the male fireflies peenies," he said. "They sail along through the air in great circles and half circles, trying to entertain the females who sit on leaves and blink. We call the female blinkies for that reason."

"So those are the two kinds of fireflies on the island of Jamaica," Laura said.

The man shook his head. "There are 50 kinds of fireflies here."

Then, "My name is Oliphant." He extended his knuckles and we brushed ours against his.

"I am marooned here," he said, stirring the fire with a piece of stick-wood.

"How so?" I asked.

"You see the house there?"

I nodded. "I see it."

"Looks like a ship, doesn't it?"

"Not exactly."

"Well, it is so. I am the captain of that ship."

He sighed and stirred the firecoals. Sparks mingled in the air with the fast moving peenies and unmoving, or slow rising and falling, blinkies.

"You see," he said, in a voice just above a whisper, "at any time we can be erased from this earth we dearly love. I was given this wrecked ship, but only for a time. A time that has, like all time, no measure. I come from the island of Guadalupe. My ancestors are from East Africa and in my place of origin, the obeahmen live outside the village."

"Is that what you are, an obeahman?"

He smiled, nodded, stirred the fire.

"I practice what I know," he said.

"To help others?" Laura inquired.

His eyes grew into thin slits. "Sometimes."

"To do harm other times?" Laura asked.

"Sometimes."

Then he explained. "The obeahman lived outside the village during times of peace. But during times of war, he lived close, inside."

"You mean inside the village walls?"

He said, "That is so."

Then, most strange, he added, "It is like a flashlight in a safe. It turns on when needed. It shuts off when not."

"Obeah is black magic," I mentioned. "As far as I know."

"What did Sungazer say it was?" he asked.

"He never told me."

"He comes to me in dreams," Oliphant said, "and asks if you have given the feathers to me. May I see them?"

I said, "He told me you would identify yourself with a story."

"Have I not done so?"

"The peenywallies are not a story."

He laughed then, but it was more a cackle than a laugh.

"Very well," he went on, "You want a story and I will tell one. Two boys from the island went down the seaside and they found a place we call a blowhole. That is where the sea goes out and in. When it withdraws, it builds up a pressure. A very great pressure. Enough to kill a man. We call the blowhole between Ochy and here, the Devil's Purse. That is because there is gold hidden there. Old, old pirate doubloons. I have seen them. They are real. So, one time the two boys dared each other to get down deep into the Devil's Purse, and steal his gold. But, as I am saying, you only have a few minutes to try this. You must lower yourself into the blowhole, grab the gold, and get out before the sea pressure explodes. If you're down there when the spume hits, you're a deadman. Or boy."

He cackled, and continued with the story. The firepit seemed to be listening: it too cackled and crackled, and we could see Oliphant's face very clearly. He could have been a woman, not a man, and his features were neither old nor young. He had no definite age on him. He could have been a boy.

"So, as I was saying, the story goes…the one boy, the younger brother was lowered into the blowhole by a rope that his older brother dropped, hand over hand, until the younger one had his feet on the coral rock. The youngster saw the bright gleam of the Devil's Purse, the doubloons shining momentarily in a beam of sunlight. He had but seconds. He snatched one big golden doubloon before his brother started pulling him out of there."

Oliphant said nothing then. He became absorbed by the black pot of brew that was bubbling and smoking over the firepit. Finally, he said, "The young boy made it to safety before the salt geyser exploded with a force strong enough to shatter his bones. That night, the boy with the gold coin slept next to his older brother and he had his hand clasped over that coin and he squeezed it all night long. In the night both boys heard the Devil calling for his treasure. His voice was the wind from the north, scraping the tall, dry-leaved Panama palms. But in the morning, he still had the coin. The only thing was, his older brother was gone, and he, the young one, was old, old, old. He had turned to wrinkles and bones."

Oliphant stopped talking. He stared into the slowly dying flames.

"What happened to the boy?" I asked after a long silence.

The fire was almost out. It was smoking.

"The boy?" he said, coming out of his trance.

"The boy," I replied. "Did he die?"

Oliphant said in a very soft voice. "He lives."

The fire sprang up one last time.

In that moment, we saw Oliphant's face.

He was a man of many, many years.

An old, old man with bony hands.

And then the flames turned to orange coals and the smoke obscured Oliphant's face, and I reached under my shirt and gave him the medicine bag with the downy prayer feathers in it and the one green feather that was the crucial one Sungazer gave me to give to him.

Chapter Thirty-Nine

The next morning I saw Mackie and his son, Junior, sitting under a Casuarina tree looking down at the beach.

Below them, glinting in the sun, there was a long cylindrical object.

"What is that?" I asked Mackie.

"One a dem bomb dem," he answered in patois.

I saw what he meant. It looked like a large torpedo.

A boy on a bicycle went by on the road above us and Mackie called to him. "Bwoi, me find one a dem bomb. Tell Police come here quick-quick."

The boy nodded and sailed down the hill to Port Maria.

"Is that a loaded bomb?" I asked Mackie.

He said, "Fully armed."

"Where from?"

"Some seh U.S. Navy. Some seh Devil. Some seh UFO."

He shrugged. "Me no know."

"Devil?" Junior asked.

Mackie said, "All blessing come from on high. Therefore, all blessing come from de Faddeh of creation."

"All ting come from de Faddeh. But Bomb must come from de Devil."

The reasoning continued as a Land Cruiser nosed its square grille over the hill above us. Four well-groomed officers of the law got out and down to where we were talking. They wore the traditional dark blue trousers with the red stripe on the side. Their pinstripe, short sleeve shirts were crisply ironed with cassava starch. There were two men and they both squatted down in front of Mackie and Junior.

Mackie's eyes went from the bomb to the officers.

"So wha ya gwine do wid dis ting, mon?" Mackie asked.

The wind blew from Hurricane Allen Point to the headland where all of us squatted and considered.

The senior officer said, "You mus carry-come down a station, sah."

"Me?" Mackie's eyebrows raised.

The officer looked toward the sea.

"Wha the mon seh fi do?" Mackie asked the other policeman.

"Mon seh fi you bring down a station house."

"Not me work dis," Mackie said.

The senior officer seemed to think about this. Then, "Listen me, mon. Ya see dat bwoi on de bike?"

Mackie said, "Me see him all de while, sah."

"You tell him tek bomb down to Military. No police job dis."

The boy shook his head. "Me ride all a way fi Military wid bomb on a me back?"

"Yah, mon, ya hear good. Go!"

It was an order. But the boy made a face, hopped on his bike, went down the road and disappeared.

Mackie stood up and yawned. Ignoring the police, he went down the old stone stairs to the sea. The bomb was right in front of him. He bent down, raised it up on his shoulder and trudged back up the stairs to the landing. Then he grasped the propeller end of the bomb and the rounded front end, and with both hands heaved it into the air.

It landed with a big splash in the sea water. For a while the cylinder pitched in the incoming tide. Then the tide took it out toward the reef.

The Port Maria policemen drove away in their Land Cruiser.

Mackie looked at Junior and laughed.

"So," he said in that deep voice of his, "Faddeh mek we gift. Me return unopen."

Junior said, "How you know it not blow us to heaven?"

Mackie shook his head. "He who walk uprightly live for-I-ver."

"Including mon who carry bomb?"

"Bob Marley tell me once, "Righteousness cover the earth as a water cover the sea."

Chapter Forty

The co-owner of Blue Harbour, Mike Gleeson, showed up to see how things were going and he found The Israel sort of running things. He said to me, "As soon as I kick this guy out of here, we're going to Club Calypso to see what the girls look like upside down."

It was a long day. Mike had his hands full. The Israel disappeared for a while and Mike got into a crazy furor of work, knocking down termite-infested fences, painting porches, cleaning the algae walls off the second Sir Noel pool below the main house. Mostly though he got Benji and Roy to do these chores while he ran around with that unlimited energy he had.

There were a thousand renovations and Mike made a great and noisy show of doing them, but much of it was hocus pocus. He whirled about like Mickey Mouse in *Fantasia*. Off and on, he had half of Port Maria scrubbing, painting, and re-building.

Laura and I watched with great amusement. Locals liked Mike. He was a laugh-a-minute kind of guy. But he was also a no-tolerance sort of boss when it came to things like a box of purloined Fab. I'll explain.

There was a worker named Skinhead, a daffy, earnest thief if there ever was one. Skinhead was a thief, a tiefmon, and everybody knew it. He was a blue-eyed halfwit whose family was part East Indian. He thought things that belonged to other people really belonged to him.

We saw him put a new box of Fab laundry detergent in his backpack one day and a new box of Tide the following day.

Mike caught him, screamed at him, kicked him off the property, and banned him from ever coming back.

What that meant was that Skinhead snuck back at night, clever little mongoose that he was, and made off with anything that wasn't nailed down.

I asked Mike, "Why do you mess with a guy who's been in prison for murder?"

Mike answered, "Because if I catch him again with a box of Fab I'm going to cut his nuts off with this machete."

Skinhead valued his nuts and stayed away.

Mike was adamant that we attend the Calypso Club night festivity, and we went along with him. It's difficult to explain Mike. I had known him for a number of years in Questa, New Mexico. Mike was a doctor of Anthropology at UCLA. He team-taught with Carlos Castaneda. He was a lopsided, ingenious thinker whose education was superior to just about everyone I knew.

He had two PhDs really, one was in pharmacological and hallucinogenic herbs of South America, which meant *drugs*. With, or because of, that doctoral thesis and his many visits to the lands that grew herbal remedies, Mike knew a lot about healing and the holiness of mythology.

That said, Laura and I accompanied Mike to the Calypso Club.

Right away Mike proceeded to get smashed.

We sipped coconut water and rum. Slowly.

Mike threw back drinks like he threw over people he didn't agree with.

After a while we couldn't find Mike.

There was a stage where some very young, attractive Jamaican girls danced provocatively.

I call it dancing but it was something out of a scene from *Star Wars*.

The girls wore tube socks. White knee-high athletic socks with blue or red colored bands across the top, the kind that soccer players might wear.

They either wore spandex short-shorts or bikini bottoms and tank tops.

The girls stared straight ahead like zombies with no expression at all —just blank eyed. They were robotic, hip moving, teenagers who did a thing called the whine, or the tiny whiney dance.

Some girls *twerked*—butt pumping hip action that appeared to set them off into odd, dead-eyed orgasms. Their shorts were wet in front but the frozen faces never changed, as they did this weird rock and roll hip tick, while at the same time, the music rolled over and under them like the pounding waters of the falls at Ocho Rios.

Then, just when we thought we'd seen everything, the girls flipped onto their heads and spun. It reminded me of break dancing but even more dangerous because the somersault, head-landing was hard and fast, and the spin looked dangerous at the edge of the small stage.

After another coconut rum, we were on the back streets of the Banana Road heading home to Blue Harbour, minus Mike, who seemed to have linked up with one of the headtop dancers.

Or not. Who knew? Mike was Mike. A street kid himself who, though grown up, married and responsible, still remembered the dogtag he had to wear as a kid. Stamped on the tag was the address where he lived and a statement that said he wasn't homeless but had no parental guardians. He was a homeless kid with a home. But no one to look after him because his father was a wandering drunk, his mother was deranged, and his brothers and sisters were fending for themselves just like Mike.

Mike was an extraordinary college professor. On the side he delivered herb to none other than Bob Marley and the Wailers.

He wrote brilliantly, and was a devout, if sometimes unreliable, friend. There wasn't much he didn't know about the culture of the Caribbean. He'd lived it, written it, married it, and run it as a hotel. Laura and I had a great fondness for him.

But we did worry about him, because down at old Blue Harbour, he tended to buy cases of Red Stripe beer just for personal use. A case at night, empty at dawn.

And, you're probably wondering about the Israel...

Laura and I saw the clash coming. As it turned out when we got back to Blue Harbour, Mike was there, really drunk, and The Israel, who'd been a trained officer in The Israel Army, was having it out with him.

They weren't at the point of throwing blows yet, but almost.

I sidled up to Roy at the bar and asked, "How long before one of them kills the other?"

Roy shook his dreadlocks, snorted. "Me end it now," he said.

Roy was tall and muscular. He had a warrior's barrel chest and strong arms. But I'd seen The Israel practicing some odd form of self-defense under the banana leaves. It was a kind of dance and chop, leap and whirl sort of Ninja thing. In my mind, I saw Roy and Mike lying on their backs with X's for eyes. The night could easily end up like that.

But Roy didn't see it that way.

"The Israel him bluff his way in 'ere. Me biff him way out."

I looked down by Roy's hip and saw that he had his right hand around an iron pipe. Roy lifted himself up, quiet as a cat, and padded into the middle of Mike and The Israel.

It happened so fast. Using his elbows, Roy separated both men, giving himself a little room.

Then he hit The Israel on the top of his head. We all heard a noise that is hard to describe. A sort of bell-like, bong-sound.

The Israel dropped like a broken building.

Mike said, "Thanks, Roy. I'm going to bed."

That was the end of it.

Two Jamaicans at the bar dragged the unconscious Israel across the cement floor of the bar and then they carried him down to Villa Rose.

The party broke up fast after that. The guys at the bar left. The lanterns glowing under the thatch roof of the bar swung musically in the wind. The night was suddenly quiet. Even the croakers were still.

We walked down to Villa Rose to see if The Israel was dead or alive.

Roy went with us. "Me knock 'im good," he said. "Him nuh wake for a good long while."

He was spread eagle on the pine plank floor.

His eyes were open. But he was out cold.

"Him nuh dead," Roy said, listening close to his open mouth.

I gently closed The Israel's eyes.

"He's going to have a real hangover in the morning," Laura said.

We left him there lying on the floor with all his money, currencies from all over the world, blowing fitfully about in skirls. The wind was up from the sea but it looked like invisible Erzulie was playing a paper money game.

"No one take it," Roy said with a sly smile.

Then he added, "Gangster money dat."

Chapter Forty-One

The following day I was in Port Maria doing the daily round of bakery, supermarket, outdoor market and so on, when a small ragamuffin man came up to me and stuck a sharp machete into my stomach.

I felt the point of the blade nick me, and stick me. But it did not go in any deeper. Still, there was a drop of blood on my t-shirt. The man held me with his eyes. The eyes were focused on mine. For a moment we held one another in that strange embrace of pure eye contact and the point of a machete.

There are times like these where you don't think, you don't act, but you can feel that something is going to happen any second, and then it does…

My mouth opened, and words poured out of it.

"I am told you are a kind and gentle soul," I said. "Why is it, all these years have passed, and we have only just met, man to man, heart to heart?"

The hardness of his eyes changed.

I went on. "I haven't an answer any more than you have an answer for the thing you are doing, pushing a knife into the belly of your brother." (I don't know—to this day—where these strange words came from.)

But for a while our duel of stares continued. Then the knife man dropped the point of his machete. His eyes filled with tears, he turned and fled. But not without saying that I was "A kind and gracious sir, a gentleman and many other nice things."

I watched him weave his way into the thickening crowd that thought a murder was going to be committed. There was a hunger in their eyes. But someone said, "You stood your ground…"

When I told what had happened to Mackie, he said, "Everyone got something to say, even a madman. But most mad people are hungry. Hungry for food. Hungry for love. Hungry for something. We walk a thin line between the quick and the dead. The starved and the sated. The rich and the poor. The real question is which do you live in, heaven or hell?"

Jamaica, it seems to me, is a place where you are proving yourself every day. There is always some forthcoming challenge around the corner, waiting for you to stand up and be counted.

In my case, these challenges often came by way of water.

After running into Runaway, so to say, I ran into a fisherman who was selling a string of snapper at the back door of the kitchen. We got into a conversation and I asked him how he got the scar that ran like lightning down the side of his face. At first, I thought it was a curved telephone scar, the kind you get in Jamaica for talking too much to the wrong people.

"No, mon," he said, "Me get dis one from a barra."

A barra, I knew, was a barracuda.

"Him rip you good," I said.

"Him tear me mask off a me face. Then him taste me face-bone."

"Him no like?"

"No, mon, him no like me face fi nyam."

He said face like "fay-ess" which seemed to me to have a rip in it.

Then, that same afternoon, while I was trolling off Reef Point, I saw that same disappointed barra. The locals said he patrolled that vicinity, and there I was, fresh meat.

A new fay-ess on the water block.

I know from diving experiences in the Caribbean never to turn full counter and swim away. Always stay within sight of that which stalks. Swim backwards if you have to, but go slow.

I finned slowly in reverse, using my hands to back paddle.

Then I saw the danger I was in. This dark stripe barra was six feet long and he was coming toward me, steady as she goes, an imperturbable force of nature.

I glanced at my hands.

I was wearing two Pueblo silver rings and one Navajo turquoise, all of which seemed to catch the barra's eye.

The great fish saw the rings, was attracted to them, came near.

I continued to back paddle, very slowly.

The barra was turned mouth forward, so all I could see now were its needle-point teeth.

The silver torpedo came closer.

He turned so I could see his right side, riddled with scars.

Batttler, monster. This hungry predator could saw me apart in a matter of minutes.

I kept backing up. I wanted to turn my head and measure the shoreline from where I was. I couldn't be too far from it now. But there was another factor. Barras will tear you apart in very shallow water.

His large moon eye held me fast.

Then I saw the vapor trail of fine white sand coming up under him.

I knew then we were in shallow water.

He came on. His yellow pectorals fanning with anticipation.

I had but one trick.

Days before I read about a man who was attacked by a grizzly bear and as the bear came at him, he lofted his arms, spread his legs, puffed out his belly and generally made himself bigger than he was. The bear threw on the brakes. It didn't like the increased size of its quarry. It pawed the earth, turned tail, and left the trail.

Now, as the giant fish came toward me, closer and closer, I took a deep breath through my snorkel, and bellied out my gut. I raised my arms until they were far apart on either side of me. Then I spread my legs as far as they would go.

I imagined that I looked like Leonardi DaVinci's cosmic man.

The barra turned in a sort of meditative circle, considering options of attack, I supposed.

I was bigger than that fish. That's all I knew.

I held the pose.

As the barra went south and then north, circling and thinking, I saw the strangeness of the creature and knew why it was so cautious.

It had only one eye.

By now I could feel the sand stirring under my fins. A cloud of smoky white silt began to fill the spaces between my legs. I took a quick look below. Suddenly I was the vague beast, all white smoke and big armed.

The barra had no wish to fight; only to eat.

He turned tail.

I scuttled, crabwise, to the silver sands of Reef Pointe.

For a while I listened to my heart drumming in my chest.

In my head I heard, "From the rivers of Babylon". Then, finally, I got up and looked around. I was in a tiny cove surrounded by a landward cliff.

At the very top of the cliff I saw a man waving to me.

It was Oliphant.

He was showing me the hand-carved path through the limestone ridges that led to his dilapidated mansion. He had little green, blue feathers hanging around his neck in a twined, hemp necklace.

I unloosed my fins and pushed my mask high on my head. Then I trudged upward.

Heaven was up, not down.

Chapter Forty-Two

Good news, bad news.

The bad came hard.

It was a call to come back to Florida. I was to meet Mr M.

My best story, the one I had the most feeling for, was about the necromancer, Oliphant.

Len liked it, Mr M didn't.

"We want something different. We have a lead on something you will be writing with another author. Someone you will meet when you get here. We have you booked on Air Jamaica Flight 1512, tomorrow noon."

Is this what happens when your life is spared by a barracuda?

We, Laura and I, had both slipped deeply into the Jamaican dreamtime.

I had imagined that I was Ian Fleming writing James Bond novels at the famed estate, Goldeneye.

In truth, we'd gone there and looked at Fleming's two-cornered desk away from the windows, set in prison-like austerity in a small room. So, I thought, that's how he wrote my favorite Jamaican novels. He'd dreamed them in a dire corner jail.

Now we were suddenly packing to leave.

At the same time, Mackie had disappeared. No one knew where he was.

I couldn't bear the thought of disappearing without saying goodbye to my mystic mentor and friend, Mackie.

But I also didn't want to lose my job.

While we packed odds and ends into a deep and wide pandana hamper, we thought about how this one month had passed in seconds. And now it was a lifetime crammed into a hand-woven pandana hamper. The maker was a man from the hills by the name of Killankully.

Somehow, word got around that we were leaving abruptly for work, and one after another, Rastas showed up to say goodbye. We had no idea we had so many friends. For the rest of that day, they showed up with small gifts that Laura tucked into the hamper.

But no Mackie.

Mike came upstairs where we were packing and asked to read the stories I'd written about Blue Harbour. He sat in the new wicker rocking chair made by Killankully and read one story after another. A few were unpublished. But he read and chuckled all the way through the manuscript.

At the end, he looked up at me and said, "Carlos would love this stuff. I think it's great. Right in line with old man Naipaul, my other teacher, and as I say, up there too with Carlos the mystic man."

He gave us each a hug and said, "You're in the firmament. Stay there."

"Where are you going?" I asked.

I could feel his wild Irish eyes pulling away from me.

"I might miss you," he said. You're leaving…when?"

"Tomorrow, early."

"I won't be back in time to see you off then. But we'll be in touch up in Taos. It's all a moveable feast as Hemingway said."

I sat on the long swinging couch for a long time. I was holding an ironwood bust of Makeda, the oft-called, Queen of Sheba. It was carved by a tuck shop man named Jah Son. Suddenly I heard Bob Marley's voice on the reggae radio station IRIE FM.

"Music is music," Marley said. "You can think of things great and you can think of things simple. You know what I mean? People see images of us and say 'That's the Wailers, right?' But music continues, know what I mean? I don't see how you can just play one music. Marley can't know about superstitious things. I feel like I-and-I rule the earth, no care which path run this. I don't have no fear about anywhere. Because if something can corrupt you, you're corrupted already. Material things…I don't understand plenty things people say about this. So much things people have to say. Every day I grow bigger. I mean, I grow larger through experience. I have seven children and I have to take care of them. You know they say gather the flock. I don't want to say it's a big thing, like Moses and thing. But all I do is beg Jah for work to do…and I do it…and I'm free."

***

Hearing this, I thought, and then said to Laura, "The same is true for us. We don't want to leave the island but we have to leave the island because we have a work to do, as they say."

And so we left on schedule the following morning, down the Ochy road with Ernie at the wheel—no Mackie—and we were on time and on board Air Jamaica before noon.

But, a few minutes before boarding, we were standing in line and Jamaica, or Jamdown, as they say, had one more thing to say.

A big fat banana slug slipped off my backpack and smacked down on the tiled floor of the airport.

I tried to get it out of harm's way.

But a fast-moving man, stepped on it, skidded, fell with his suitcase.

"Did Jah mean that to be?" I asked Ernie.

"Ya mon, him mean that, too."

Chapter Forty-Three

At Miami International Airport, Laura was pick-pocketed.

All of our American Express Travelers checks were stolen, plus her new Lenscrafters glasses, some keys, and a cigarette lighter.

The sleight-of-hand man—and I did see it was a man—melted into the crowd. Vanished in a sea of heads, hats, and typical, colorful, Miami miasma.

Laura said, "I actually felt his hand dip and dive. But he was so quick and his hand was so light, I thought my purse was brushed by the person next to me."

"Well, actually, it was," I said. "You were marked. In Jamaica, you know, they'd run and catch the guy and mark him."

"In this crowd?"

"Well, maybe not."

After she went through her purse, we walked to an airport phone and called American Express. While she was talking to a representative, I felt in my pocket for the Sungazer crystal. It was still there.

New AMEX Traveler's Checks would be issued in Marco, no problem, but the prescription glasses were a loss and so were the New Mexico house keys.

Around two and a half hours later, we were in a restaurant called The House of Blue Lights. Len had reserved a table, and there was also a surprise mystery guest.

Lo and behold, our old ufologist friend, Etienne.

"What are *you* doing here?"

He stood up, we hugged, and he did that French thing of kissing both cheeks.

"It's been some time," he said quietly, sitting down. Then, "As you see me, I am on assignment…thanks to this gentleman here." He gestured to a stranger who walked up to our table and sat down next to Len.

"Hello," the stranger said. "You don't know me but I am your finicky boss, Matt Madson. You call me Mr M, right?"

Laura and I laughed.

I said, "First we get robbed in Miami. Then we meet the invisible Mr M and our old friend Etienne. Anyone else in the wings?"

"No one you'd know…yet," Mr M said.

Fried clam sandwiches, iced coffee and salad helped to put a veneer on the surprise and the culture shock. It's odd to say that coming back to the place where you are most familiar is a shock but Jamaica is the only place I've ever been where coming home to the U.S. is the shock of a lifetime.

Mr M grinned. He was a short, round, large-eared man with great moist eyes.

"So you two, you'll be working with your old confrère, if I may borrow a brotherly word from the French."

"When you say, 'you two' you must mean Laura and me."

Mr M smiled, nodded, patted Etienne on the shoulder.

"I mean, let's face it," Len Coppard put in, "two old pros working with another old pro. What could be better than that?"

It was the truth, for sure. Laura and I wrote children's books together and some adult titles, too. Etienne had worked on assignment back in the old UFO days in the 70s. I was reeling from the euphoria, the make-believe suddenness of it all. Was all of this really happening?

At the end of our editorial meeting, we learned that Etienne had made a discovery off the shores of Pine Island, just north of Marco. Someone had uncovered a rare artifact on a shell mound. A golden cat. A priceless

Calusa Indian figure that was now housed in a museum. Etienne, Laura and I would be the first to interview the "finder."

This was almost too much to believe. Etienne. The Calusa Cat. Being back in the homeland, getting robbed, having lunch in a fast-serving, upscale Marco Island restaurant surrounded by rich white people. It was daunting, if not flaunting. I found that my hands trembled. They were, at least, my hands. They weren't hairy creature hands. They were the clean hands of a typist. Ah, it was all a bit confusing.

In the men's room, washing said hands, I got another surprise.

M sidled up to me and said, "Recognize me?"

I turned sideways and looked at him.

"I recognize the tone of your voice. It's somehow like the emails I've gotten from you."

"Those were written by Len. Maybe I put in a word or two."

"I'm confused. Did we meet before I went to Jamaica?"

Mr M burst out laughing. "What do you think M stands for anyway?"

I said, "Madson?"

"Use your imagination, then look again into my eyes."

I did that thing. I still didn't recognize him.

He shook his head, while drying his hands with a paper towel.

"You met me, originally, through Etienne," he explained.

"Al-lan?" I said, leaning against the tiled bathroom wall.

"That's me. But here I'm called Mu. You know the Chinese word for emptiness. Americans spell it Moo. Well, that fits, too, as you yourself know. I still work for the Xerxians. You do, too. Is that more information than you can handle?"

"You were a cool cow, Al-lan. Is it okay if I call you that now?"

"Keep it quiet," he said. "Al-lan is a wanted man. This new disguise as a mild-mannered editor fits better, I think. Anyway, the Annexerians can't seem to find me here. So I'm safe. It got a bit tense in Jamaica when the farmer tried to sell me at the farmer's market in Highgate."

"How did you get away?"

"Did you ever hear of mad cow disease?" I kicked them all round the place and got away into the hills. There I bit the ticks off me and by night I changed into an old penner, you know one of those dingy old herdsmen with a rawhide whip and tall boots. So I left my cowskin in a hollow tree and came here back here to the states."

I scratched my head. "This is better fiction than you'd find in a novel, Al-lan."

"Let's not use that name. See the guy over there taking a piss? He's all ears."

Chapter Forty-Four

Now I understood why the five-named Al-lan, also known as Moo, Mu, Mr Madson, and Mr M, liked my stories. They were his stories. Maybe he was writing them, not me. At any rate, Jamaica was behind me, Mackie was missing, Al-lan was here…and where was I?

Etienne and I drove to Pine Island and had a look around. Laura stayed on Marco. "I don't want any part of this adventure," she said. "I'll stay here with our things."

It was just a day trip. Etienne and I went to the Randall Museum to see the cat. The carved wooden effigy from five hundred years ago.

"Can you hand tremble into the cat?" he asked me.

I shrugged. It was under glass lying on a bed of mallow grass. The effect was that as an observer you felt you had discovered it yourself. There it was—a creature from another dimension. The grain in the wood looked like veins. The serene cat face was female, or so it seemed to me. The body, too. Long and lithe, narrow shouldered, widening at the hip. She was kneeling with her paws resting on her lithesome thighs.

Again, I got a little chill, realizing that this feline being was an alien from the present, not the past. Could it be a creature of code? A message from the past, telling us that the future was comprised of non-human beings of a supernatural order?

And this was the future.

"Can you enter its mind?" Etienne persisted.

"I'm trying," I said.

Visitors to the museum were bumbling about, talking. I could hear some fish crows outdoors, grawking. I was still jet-lagged, or travel-bummed. I felt raw and under the weather. How could I—and then it happened. I was in another world. I was with the girl who had discovered the cat in the mangrove mud of a tiny island in the Pine Island Sound...

It was after 7:00 when we found Crying Key—so-called because they say you can hear ghosts wailing there at night. Beyond that, Little Clam Key. Then Frank found anchorage on an oyster bar right in front of Coon Key. Overhead the frigate birds were flying. Pelicans were diving. The water was full of jumping mullet and crashing pelicans.

Frank said, "Like Red told us, the Indian Mound's just inshore of here." He tied the runabout to a mangrove root.

"—Said we'd see his diggings," Dana remembered.

Up from the mangroves they found a hill carpeted in pine needles. It started to rain. Little fine points of wetness that tickled the skin. Frank was the first to see it, but whether it was a wild hog's rooting ground or the real thing—Red's mound digging—he wasn't sure.

Turned out, it was both.

Piles of shells, sticky and goopy, everywhere. Cloven hog prints tooled into the mud. Red's soppy old cigarette butts. "I just cut myself on a saw palmetto," Dana complained.

J.J. and Frank didn't hear her. They were already using broken conch shells as shovels. "This is so against the law," Dana told them, dabbing some mud on her cut and looking through the mangrove leaves at the failing light. Still, though her heart was beating fast, she wouldn't have left the spot for anything.

Then her eye latched onto something.

She touched J.J.'s shoulder. "What's that?"

In the half-light, she saw a tiny gleam.

All action on the digging stopped.

The mosquitoes whined. The pelicans flapped. Mosquito hawks hummed. Herons squawked, sounding like nails yanked out of boards. Night came early to the keys.

What Dana saw was a wink of gold that lay in the midst of the headless bones of a Caloosa Indian buried before Columbus was born.

"Look," she said.

The night birds squawked. Downy nestlings peeped shrilly in the rookeries of the mangroves.

Darkness settled down.

"What is it?" Frank said, wiping the sweat from his eyes.

Dana dived down and picked the twinking thing up.

J.J.'s jaw fell open. "It's a...omelet," he said.

Frank laughed. "You mean, an amulet, dummy."

"What's that?" J.J. asked, swatting mosquitoes.

Dana held it up so they all could see it.

"It's a cat," she mumbled, awestruck.

A mosquito settled on her nose. She flattened it with her other hand, leaving a mud streak.

She rubbed her nose against her shoulder and smeared the mud evenly across her cheeks.

The cat had a gleam to it.

Dana parted with the cat.

Both boys felt the heft of it with their open hands.

"Whoa, I get the creeps holding it," Frank said. He gave it back to Dana. "You keep it, now."

Dana drew a deep breath. "I think it's something supernatural," she said.

Frank said, "Let's get out of here. This isn't legal, and you know what happened to Red when he came out here and stole the skull."

"I know one thing," Dana said. "Red sure didn't have a clue as to what was really buried out here."

"He thought it was just a bunch of bones," J.J. said.

"If he'd found this cat," Frank said, "he would've sold it fast and moved to a nice house on Whiskey Creek."

"So what do we do now?" J.J. asked, looking from Frank to Dana.

"Maybe we should put the cat back where we found it," Dana said.

"Back in the mud?" Frank said. "That's not right either."

"I don't know," Dana mumbled. "Maybe none of this is right. We've stumbled on something that doesn't belong to us. We're not even supposed to be here."

There was this eerie feeling she had. Like the ghost trees and the broken shells were calling for the cat, begging to have it back. She knew it wasn't possible, but the weight of it seemed to have grown, and was growing still. A cold fear clutched at her heart. She held the cat; and it seemed to have a hold on her.

Frank piloted the johnboat back to Pine Island.

The cat grew heavier and heavier in Dana's arms.

She stared at the creature.

It seemed to be smiling.

And saying, "I am alive."

She wondered, too, about the bare bones on which the cat had dreamed over the centuries.

The same bones Red had pushed aside to capture a skull that got him arrested and sent to the county jail.

A Caloosa skull.

Now the cat the once living man had held was cradled in her arms. It was warm against her body while she rode across the seaweed meadows of the tidal bay.

A manatee surfaced with the sound a snorkel makes clearing water. Some pinfish popped around the boat. Cape Haze shed its reddish luminous dome of light as she and the boys droned on.

That night, after parting with vows to keep their secret quiet, Dana went to bed and shivered in her sleep. She'd been voted keeper of the cat by her friends. It was now lying in her sock drawer.

Was this how the world's great diggers felt when they entered a tomb that had been sealed for centuries? Was this how Columbus felt when he laid his greedy hands on Arawak gold? Did it burn his hand, too?

The girl's wandering mind returned to the cat. Its sullen, secretive face. How did it feel? Did it feel? What was it like for the cat to be apart from its owner, the skeleton in the mud of centuries.

But wood doesn't have a heart.

Or does it?

Did the cat yearn to be joined again with that frail fragment of breastbone? That man borne over the centuries on the mud banks of ancient conchs, clams, turtles and shells?

Was she going crazy?

There was a sound coming from her sock drawer.

The more she heard it, the more she knew—the cat had a heart.

More than that—it had a soul.

It was connected not just to the sea but to the stars, the circling heavens, the rounding earth, the curling cosmos, every living thing that lived and breathed.

It was alive.

Chapter Forty-Five

Mr Mu, as I now called him more often than Al-lan, liked the revised story of the Caloosa Cat. He liked it so much that he put it on the *Aquamaze* Feature Page.

Etienne and I wrote a postscript for the piece, explaining where the Cat could actually be viewed with some other details that pained us to write. Namely, that the "finder" was no longer alive.

Months after her discovery, she hanged herself from a tree. A note in her handwriting led some to believe that she suffered from bipolar depression. We thought otherwise. Was it, as she mentioned in her note, the curse of the cat? The Caloosas were a tribe killed off by Spanish influenza. They had good reason to hate their conquerors.

So concluded Etienne's and my collaborative work. We needed a rest from the magazine, Mr Mu, Len Coppard, but mostly, the sticky backwater burrows of rural Florida. If the stories needed to come from such dark and desperate roots, maybe we needed to take a break.

For a while they begged us to keep writing for them.

My excuse was that I was writing a novel and would have no time for articles about Skunk Apes and other ghostly myths of the barrier islands.

"Fine," Mr Mu said, "we'll publish it."

Then, "The Caloosa Cat" won a Best of Series Award from the American Regional Magazine Association.

I framed the award citation and hung it on our bedroom wall.

But that didn't stop the bizarre dreams of that hanging tree.

I saw it in my sleep.

Dana got a weird consolation prize, too—a named street on Pine Island. *Dana Taylor Circle.*

The hanging tree, so to say, came down in the last hurricane, or so we heard.

We stayed, Laura and I, doing some editorial odds and ends for the magazine, for a month.

Etienne got bored and returned to France.

He did, however, keep up a steady flow of articles in a French publication called *Le Mystere Mystique*. He even wrote one about me and my hand trembling gift. Etienne's insights inspired me to write a mythological study in which I not only interviewed myself, but also some Navajo friends of twenty or more years. Jimmy BlueEyes and Joogii made it clear that Diné had been doing hand trembling for hundreds of years. I did some research and traced it back to tenth century Tibet.

***

From there I went on and wrote a novel about that ancient ceremonial art. The Navajos used it to reveal "that which he knows" —which, in a sense, he didn't know until the tremble took place.

For me, hand trembling, as in moving from one body to another is both psychologically and physically dangerous. Some people who do it don't return. Some come back broken. Leave it, I say now, to the medicine men.

I stopped doing it because I began to feel the stress of it. Days after I'd come back from the precarious skin of some other being, I was nerve-wracked and shaky. The last time I disappeared into a wolf, I came back with an aneurism, a blood clot.

Further, I have never known for sure if I truly went to a place, or if, in a sense, the nature of the place came to me. I was no longer hairy-handed, but the strength in my hands is still there. I can still crush walnuts. Then again my great aunt at 100 could do the same. Maybe it's a gift. Maybe not. She used it to cane New England antique chairs for a living. I used it to write stories.

Once, before I left the magazine altogether, Mr Mu paid me a princely sum to take him into the Navajo underworld.

Forgive the fragmented images. The only way I was able to retrieve the odyssey was through the process of a running nerve-movie in my mind where the events streamed before my inner eye in a phantasmagorical blur.

Chapter Forty-Six

You visualize the hole in the rock. Traveling through it will lead you to the third, second and first world.

You are going backwards in time.
Back to the worlds of beetles, bats, and monsters.

You arrive in the world of the Holy People.
Those who ride on sunbeams.
Ride on lightning bolts.
Walk on rainbows.

If you travel back to the first world, all the people are creatures.
But it is dark there, no plants, not even any stones.
There are no Earth Surface People.
Moving upward then, you see the second world, and there is more light.

You meet First Man, First Woman, First Girl, First Boy, Coyote and Fire God.

In this second world, you feel within you the first elements.
There is a trembling of rain, but it is more an urge than a thing you can touch or feel. It starts in the center of your belly and spreads out as rain will do, but as yet there is no rain. No sun.

You continue to move upward toward a tiny little crack of light.

You crawl with all the many-legged insect people and the others who are two-legged, four-legged, no legged, and you find yourself at the top of a mountain.

Not until you reach the fifth world above the mountain of mist do you find you have a heart.

With that discovery comes day and night. You come to know the power of light and dark and you hold both within you, and you call them good and evil.

You make love with a coyote maiden and this causes a coyote man to steal Water Monster's babies and this brings on the Great Flood.

You have sacred stones loaned to you by First Man.

You have Whiteshell, Turquoise, Abalone, Jet and Red-white Stone.

You have powers that can even overcome Coyote, the mischief maker.

You see the coming of the great waters that rise and rise and cover the earth.

You feel the discord between man and woman, and as the changes come, Woman moves away from Man and has sex with herself and the person known as Cholla.

You see that this separation brings on the Monsters that will now inhabit the earth.

You understand that Changing Woman has also had sex with one of the Holy People and when she gives birth to the Monster Slayers, a new world begins to open up to all creatures large and little, two-legged, four-legged, many-legged, no legged.

You know that from the body of Changing Woman comes a new race of beings called Diné, The People.

You see the monsters are slain by the two brothers of the Sun, the monster blood turns into red sand, dark sand, black sand, bitter water, deer spring, popping leaves, falling leaves.

All is memory.

All is woven.

All is dream.

All is trembling.

In harmony it is done.

Chapter Forty-Seven

I told Mr Mu that there wasn't much else. He'd seen it all. Experienced the whole transcendence of the Navajo five worlds.

"Is there nothing else?" he asked.

"Why do you want to go through this?"

He stroked his chin. "Well, to be perfectly honest, these worlds are the only ones that can't be decoded by the Annexerians. They can get anywhere else. They can squeeze into a tiny crack between worlds, but they can't decode worlds that don't exist."

"But as you have seen," I said, "these time spheres of the Navajo do exist. They're real. But the code can't be duplicated. Nor can it be cracked by a hacker from another universe. I've been using this Sungazer crystal, which you've seen me hold up to my eye when looking directly at the Sun."

"—And that's how you make the shift from "real time" to the Navajo medicine man's cosmology of the five worlds?"

"Yes."

"Then let's go again. It's like an amusement park ride, for me."

"That's what I was afraid of."

"What do you mean?"

"Well, if we so much as alter one blade of grass in Navajo emergence time, we can cause the Monsters to return. They've already been slain, let's leave their blood sand where it belongs."

"What is the most frightening thing you've experienced in this world?"

"Winter Thunder."

Mr Mu shrugged. "Winter thunder, huh. That's nothing like falling into a black hole. Thunder's child's play."

"So you say."

"Give me a shot, will you? It can't be worse than being trapped inside a cow and not remembering the combination code to get out."

"Very well," I said, but don't cry if you can't handle this."

I took the crystal out of the medicine bag and saw the face of the Sun. In a moment I heard the Night Chant from far off in my inner ear. It came and went, and came and went again. After hearing the chant nine times, I felt the transformation begin.

The words came out of my mouth like falling water, a waterfall of words.

Winter Thunder rumbled over our heads.

Suddenly the earth shook, the heavens thundered.

I heard Mr Mu say, "I can't breathe. My breath is gone from me."

I saw a shaft of light and I was in a cage of old willows.

I felt my mouth. My teeth were gone.

Twelve winds—I counted them—tore away my ribs, my pelvis, my spine.

Then, my collarbone, my tailbone.

"My bones are gone!" Mr Mu said. He too was in the willow cage.

We were like fat slugs. Boneless.

Forks of lightning came down and blasted the cage to bits of bark.

We crawled on our bellies. I could feel Mr Mu's elbows touch mine and they were pieces of sodden meat. The rain railed down on us.

I saw Mu's innards fly out of his mouth in a red vomit of fleshy things, including a beating heart spewing blood. I watched them soar and land on cactus spikes, dangling obscene in the forked lightning flash-crack.

My guts came next, a wrenching avalanche of gut filth.

We lay, both of us, ruined bags of skin.

Then out of my toothless mouth came the chant of All IS Well, which I sang nine times.

The sky seared cold blue and in whirlwinds came a storm of grass-hoppers.

Then it snowed yellow corn pollen and a hundred corn-carrying bee-tles brought back our guts and forced them into our dry mouths, one after another.

Other body parts were brought to us by bluebirds that entered us through the tips of our fingers.

I felt the cave of myself fill with body parts that then took their natural place within the thing that I call myself.

My teeth returned on the leather wings of tiny bats.

My saliva, my hair, my teeth, my fingernails—all returned.

I heard myself ask them, all of them, every single body part, "Did you like the Places of the North and Nightwind where Winter Thunder ruled?"

And all answered but my bones.

My bones refused to answer.

Chapter Forty-Eight

There were a few more shards of words to say.

But I did not say them. They issued from my mouth, but I had no control over them. More words, mine. Then his echo after me. My voice, his voice, like a soft drumbeat on the skin of the earth.

For long years I have kept this beauty within me
It has been our life
It is given like the dew
The pollen of the cornflower
My days have been long
May our days be made longer
So no harm comes
And Winter Thunder will stay away
All is beautiful
All around us, behind us, below us, above us
All is beautiful
The skies, the waters, the darkness, the dawn, the light of the Sun
Whose ways are beautiful
Whose ways are beautiful
All around us
All around us

Coming Soon!

STAR SONG *series*
Hail Chanter
Book 4
by
Gerald Hausman

In *Hail Chanter*, Jack Andrews is called upon to rescue his Xerxian friend, Al-lan, who has been captured by a cosmic arch enemy. In a strange and intriguing exchange, Al-lan is freed but Jack must travel in time to pay off Al-lan's captors by bringing them stolen sacred objects from humanity's past. In doing so, Jack himself is rescued by his old mentor, Stargazer. The only way to put things right is a Hail Chant delivered by a ghost.

An SV Original Publication

For more information
visit: www.SpeakingVolumes.us

Now Available

STAR SONG *series*
Books 1 - 2

For more information
visit: www.SpeakingVolumes.us

Now Available

"A must read. If you haven't yet read it, get it.
It's a fine reading experience."
—Allan W. Eckert, author of *That Dark and Bloody River*

For more information
visit: www.SpeakingVolumes.us

Now Available

HOWARD MOON DEER MYSTERIES
Books 1 - 4

"Terrific…I couldn't put it down."
—Margaret Truman, author of *Murder at the Watergate*

For more information
visit: www.SpeakingVolumes.us

Now Available

SHERIFF LANSING MYSTERIES
Books 1 – 3

For more information
visit: www.SpeakingVolumes.us